"Josh!

She trie[d]
was struck [with a pain.]
She gasped, and instinctively her hand
moved to her stomach.

"Sam, what is it?"

His voice seemed to be coming from a great
distance away as another pain struck.

Her eyes lifted to his, filled with fear. "It's
the baby...Josh. I think I'm going into labor."

EXPECTING

She's sexy, successful... and PREGNANT!

Relax and enjoy our new series of stories about spirited women and gorgeous men, whose passion results in pregnancies...sometimes unexpected! Of course, the birth of a baby is always a joyful event, and we can guarantee that our characters will become besotted moms and dads—but what happened in those nine months before?

Share the surprises, emotions, dramas and suspense as our parents-to-be come to terms with the prospect of bringing a new little life into the world.... All will discover that the business of making babies brings with it the most special love of all....

KATHRYN ROSS

The Unexpected Father

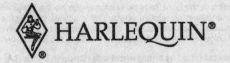

TORONTO • NEW YORK • LONDON
AMSTERDAM • PARIS • SYDNEY • HAMBURG
STOCKHOLM • ATHENS • TOKYO • MILAN • MADRID
PRAGUE • WARSAW • BUDAPEST • AUCKLAND

ISBN 0-373-12022-2

THE UNEXPECTED FATHER

First North American Publication 1999.

Copyright © 1996 by Kathryn Ross.

Printed in U.S.A.

CHAPTER ONE

WHEN Samantha found out that she was pregnant she could hardly believe it. Once she had recovered from the shock, the delight and excitement set in. Although she knew a baby would change their lives radically, she never for one moment suspected that her husband would be anything other than ecstatic about the news.

Even now, as she lay in a hospital bed drifting between consciousness and the depths of darkness, his reaction haunted her. Their marriage had been a whirlwind affair, and their relationship tenuous at times. Yet even through all the insecurities of loving Ben she hadn't been prepared for the truth. He just didn't love her. It was a bitter twist of fate that she should find out now, when she was just six weeks pregnant.

Through a mist of confusion people were saying her name over and over again, but she was too tired to open her eyes; she just wanted to sleep and sleep into oblivion. The bomb blast that had hit the hospital might have bruised and battered her, but it was nothing compared with the ache deep in her heart.

She opened her eyes once and saw a man standing beside her; he was just a hazy, blurred shadow.

'Ben?' She murmured his name, her voice sounding strange to her ears. 'Ben?'

Someone called for a nurse; it didn't sound like Ben's voice. She closed her eyes, too weak to think any more.

* * *

When she opened her eyes next it was like coming through a thick fog. Then gradually things became clearer and she could see Sister Roberts looking down at her, her expression concerned. 'How are you feeling?' she asked gently.

It took a moment even to be able to find her voice. 'As if I've been run over by a steam train,' she murmured at last. Her eyes moved past the nurse. She recognised the general care unit where she had worked for the last two years, though now she was viewing it from a very unfamiliar angle. She tried to sit up, and winced as pain shot through her body.

'Don't try to move.' Sister Roberts put a gentle hand on her shoulder.

'I don't think I can.' Samantha swallowed rawly. Then her eyes sought the nurse's anxiously. 'Am I still pregnant? Is...is my baby all right?' She held her breath as she waited for the woman to answer.

The sister nodded. 'Perfectly all right...you were very lucky.'

A wave of relief washed through Samantha's body. If Ben had previously given her any doubts about whether or not she wanted this baby, they were gone for ever now. She wanted her baby with all her heart; that much was certain.

'Try and get some rest,' the sister urged as she watched a tear trickle down the girl's cheek. 'You are badly bruised but there is no permanent damage.'

Samantha shook her head restlessly. She could hear the distant sound of gunfire—not an unusual sound in the remote African township of Chuanga. For four years now civil war had torn the beautiful little country of Nuangar apart. Samantha had been here with the aid agency for two and a half years, but she still hadn't got used to the tragic futility of it all.

'What happened?' Her voice was hoarse and strained as she remembered the direct attack on the hospital—the first of its kind. 'I remember running through the ward and out into the corridor to see what was happening, then the explosion...' Her voice wavered alarmingly at the memory. 'Were many people killed...? Where's Ben...is Ben all right?'

'We'll talk about Ben later...when you're feeling stronger.'

Cold, clammy hands felt as if they were squeezing Samantha's heart as she looked up at the woman. She had been a nurse for too long not to recognise the expression in her colleague's eyes, in her voice.

Regardless of the pain, she hoisted herself up from the pillows. 'Ben's dead...isn't he?' Her voice wobbled precariously.

The sister hesitated before answering truthfully. 'The ward he was working in got a direct hit, Sam... He wouldn't have known any pain.'

For a moment Samantha seemed to take the news stoically, then she collapsed back against the bed.

Josh watched the sleeping woman with a deep, brooding gaze. Something about Samantha Walker got to him. He couldn't have said what it was...the air of vulnerability...the fragile, almost ethereal beauty...just something about her.

His eyes moved over the pallor of her skin, made even paler by the mass of dark hair that framed the delicate oval of her face. She had incredibly long dark lashes, and soft lips that were tinged with gentle colour. In sleep she had a childlike, extremely vulnerable quality about her.

She moved in a fretful way and murmured something incoherently. Then suddenly she looked directly at him.

Her eyes were an unusual shade of deep hyacinth-blue,

an arresting contrast with the darkness of her hair. There was confusion in the wide gaze. 'Ben?' she murmured, her voice husky with sleep.

'It's Josh.' He corrected her gently. 'Josh Hamilton.'

Her eyes closed and he thought she had drifted back to sleep again. He was surprised, therefore, when she spoke quite clearly to him after a moment's silence, an edge of derision in her voice. 'Oh, it's you.'

'There's no need to sound quite so disappointed,' he answered laconically.

'You mean you want me to sound grateful?' She couldn't help the bitter note, though why she felt so strongly against this man she couldn't have said. She had met him only once, just before the bomb blast that had destroyed part of the hospital. According to Sister Roberts, he had risked his life to save hers. She should say some words of thanks.

'I'm not here for gratitude,' he said abruptly. 'I just wanted to see if you were all right. I thought I owed Ben that much at least.'

Guilt flooded through her. She lifted her eyes and looked up at him again. 'I'm sorry...I do appreciate what you did.'

He waved her words aside impatiently. 'I told you, I'm not here for that.'

Her gaze moved over the darkness of his hair and the tanned, rugged contours of his face. He had light green eyes, she noticed absently, and his lithe frame was powerfully built. He seemed to personify the outdoor, strongly masculine type. Perhaps it was that aura of strength that unnerved her so much.

'Sister tells me that you have been in to see me nearly every day.' She pushed her hair away from her face with a self-conscious hand. 'Haven't you anything better to do?' She wondered if that had sounded rude. She hadn't

meant it to, it was just that she felt disconcerted by Josh
Hamilton's presence. The knowledge that he had sat next
to her while she slept made her feel embarrassed; she
didn't like the thought that he might have watched her
closely while her defences were down. 'I thought you
were a busy reporter who was in a hurry to get out of this
place.'

'I am.' His mouth twisted in a rueful smile. 'I should
have been out of Chuanga last week.' He held up his left
wrist, which was heavily bandaged. 'Unfortunately this
has put paid to my travelling for a while.'

'How did you do that?' She struggled to sit up further
and he stretched across with his right hand and helped her
adjust the pillow. The sudden closeness made her visibly
flinch away from him before she could check the impulse.

'All right now?' He sat back as if he hadn't noticed the
awkward moment.

'Yes, thank you.' Her voice held a slight tremor, and
for a second her eyes collided with his direct, steady gaze.
Hurriedly she looked away. For some reason Josh made
her feel completely ill at ease. 'You...you were about to
tell me how you hurt your arm. Did it happen during the
raid on the hospital?' she forced herself to continue
lightly.

He hesitated. He could have told her that it had happened when he had gone down into the debris of the hospital corridor to drag her out. Instead he shrugged. 'No—
got out of the war without a scratch.' He grinned. 'Got
this arm-wrestling with Sister Roberts...she's some lady.'

Samantha didn't smile; there was a part of her that felt
she would never laugh at anything again. She shuddered.
'I still can't believe that anyone could be so evil as to
attack a hospital.'

'It's beyond comprehension.' He hesitated before continuing gently, 'Ben will be a sad loss.'

Dark lashes closed over her eyes. She wasn't able to talk about Ben, not yet...and certainly not to Josh Hamilton.

'Samantha?' His voice was gentle.

Her eyes opened, their beauty lit by an inner light, an inner pain. 'It's OK,' she told him awkwardly, then changed the subject abruptly. 'If I hadn't delayed you that evening in the ward you would probably be back in Salanga now.'

'Maybe.' His lips curved in a wry grin. 'I knew you were trouble the minute I set eyes on you. I should have heeded my instincts.'

For a moment Samantha's mind veered back to the nightmare of that evening.

Josh had been just another patient in her ward. He had been injured on the way in to Chuanga when the supply convoy he had been travelling with had come under attack. Luckily he had escaped with just a minor wound to the side of his head.

She remembered that she had found him extremely infuriating. He had sat on the edge of his bed fully dressed, and had made it plain that he was in a hurry to get out of the place because he had a deadline to meet for a story. Samantha couldn't have cared less and had told him so in no uncertain terms.

She had been stretched to the limits of her endurance, with a full ward, a shortage of staff and a feeling of sickness curling around in her stomach. She hadn't been sure if that feeling had been due to pregnancy or the fact that her husband had told her that morning that their marriage was definitely over. Whatever it had been, she had felt that Josh Hamilton was the final weight to tip the balance of her temper.

The other nurse who had been on duty with her had

had no such reservations. She had fluttered around him, flirting with him flagrantly.

Even now the memory made Samantha cringe with embarrassment. Joanne had made it very clear that she was attracted to him and Josh had looked lazily amused, as if he was used to women throwing themselves at him.

Samantha had stopped next to them and told them in a clear, icy tone that if there had been such a thing as a bucket of cold water in Chuanga she would have thrown it over them.

Joanne had looked totally disconcerted. Josh had merely laughed, and his eyes had moved in an assessing way over Sam's slender figure with a gleam of male approval that had completely thrown her.

'Anyone ever tell you that frosty manner of yours is sexy as hell?' he had drawled outrageously.

She had known he was deliberately taunting her, and her cheeks had flared with furious colour.

'Did anyone ever tell you that there is such a thing as a common line of decency, and you have just crossed it?'

'You mean I've offended you.' He was totally unperturbed. 'Tell you what—the sooner you check the stitches on my forehead, the sooner I can be out of here and out of your way.' He gave her an exaggerated salacious wink. 'How about it?'

'I'm sorry, but no matter how outrageous you are I am not going to let you jump the queue. I have other people to attend to and so has Joanne.' She gave her colleague a meaningful look. 'Mr Hamilton will just have to wait his turn—'

'Mr Hamilton is out of here.' Josh interrupted decisively. 'I've never liked waiting in queues anyway.'

She watched him gathering up his things with a feeling of intense annoyance.

'I want to go across and have a word with Ben Walker before I leave, anyway.'

Samantha had been in the process of turning away from him.

She swung back with a frown marring her smooth features. 'What do you want to see Dr Walker for?'

'We're old friends.' He bent to put his shoes on. 'Don't worry, I'm not putting in a complaint about you,' he added with a tinge of humour.

'I'm not in the slightest bit worried.' She glared at the top of his dark head, hardly able to believe that she could feel such strong antagonism towards a total stranger. 'For one thing I'm doing my job well, for another Dr Walker is my husband.'

He straightened then, his expression incredulous. 'You are Ben Walker's wife?'

'Yes.' She met his gaze steadily.

He looked down at the wedding band on her finger as if noting it for the first time. 'He never mentioned a thing about being married,' he said after a moment. 'I spoke to him this morning for about half an hour and he didn't mention you once.'

Ordinarily Samantha would just have laughed. She had a sunny nature, and usually a smile came readily to her lips. The situation with her husband, however, had changed all that.

She couldn't say she was surprised that Ben hadn't mentioned her, but nevertheless it still hurt. 'Well, he's never mentioned you either,' she muttered sharply.

His eyes swept over her in a long, leisurely appraisal. 'Ben always did have good taste in women,' he remarked reflectively. 'Never thought he would get married, though. Didn't think he was the marrying kind.'

Those words rang hollowly inside her now. She was overwhelmed by a sudden urge to cry. Ridiculous to cry now, she told herself sternly. She hadn't cried when Ben had made his feelings clear to her. She hadn't cried when the sister had told her that Ben was dead. Now, remembering Josh Hamilton's words, she wanted to break down.

She breathed deeply. She had to get a grip, think logically. She had decisions to make—decisions that were painful.

Her head turned towards the table next to her, searching for a glass of water.

'Would you like a drink?' Josh asked immediately, stretching to pick up the glass for her.

'Thank you.' Her throat cracked slightly as she controlled the emotional storm inside.

Her fingers brushed against his as she took the glass he held out to her. Their eyes locked for a moment, then Samantha looked hastily away.

Josh was a total enigma to her. She couldn't work him out at all. Obviously he was being nice to her now because he felt sorry for her, because Ben had been his friend.

She didn't want anybody's sympathy; she certainly didn't want Josh Hamilton's. Her hand trembled badly as she held the glass. He didn't let go of it, helping her as an adult would help a child. Annoyance mixed with gratitude. She wished to hell she could understand the way she was feeling.

After a few sips she lay back against her pillow again.

A young nurse walked past them and smiled provocatively at Josh. She noticed that he returned the smile in a warm, lazy kind of way.

Samantha looked away from him. 'Don't let me detain you here.' She muttered the words abrasively. 'I'm sure you must have better things to do.'

'Am I to take it that's your way of telling me to go?' he asked sardonically.

'If you like.'

'Fine.' He stood up. He seemed to tower over her bed-side. He was tall—well over six feet. 'I hope you feel better soon.'

Her reply was interrupted by Sister Roberts as she came to check up on Samantha, her trained eye moving over the girl's pallor with concern.

'Well, how is my favourite patient today?' she asked light-heartedly.

'Not bad.' Samantha shrugged. 'When can I get up from here? I'm starting to feel as if I'm taking root in this bed.'

'You've only been there a few days,' the sister said with a shake of her head. 'You need the rest, Sam.'

'I need to get back to work...that's what I need,' Samantha said bleakly. 'You must be really short-staffed.'

'We are managing,' the sister assured her quickly.

Josh moved from the bedside. 'Well, I'll leave you two ladies to talk.' His eyes moved over Samantha's face, then he smiled. 'See you later.'

'Nice man.' Sister Roberts sat down in the chair he had vacated. 'He must have nerves of steel the way he was able to run into the hospital corridor to get you out. Parts of the roof were still falling in.'

'Was that when he hurt his arm?'

The sister nodded.

Out of the side of her eye she could see Josh speaking to the nurse who had smiled at him. Then Nurse Joanne Kelly walked over to him as well. Josh said something to them and they both laughed.

'He certainly seems to be a hit with the staff,' she said, and for some reason couldn't get rid of the asperity in her tone.

'I suppose.' Sister Roberts darted a glance over at her two members of staff. 'Anyway, I haven't come to talk about Josh Hamilton. I thought maybe you were ready to discuss what you want to do.'

'Do?' Samantha swallowed nervously.

'You are going to have to return home, Sam.' The woman's voice was gentle. 'You are in no fit state to continue working here. You are in shock and—'

'Pregnant. Dreadful combination,' Samantha said with dry humour.

'I was about to say you need peace and quiet for a while,' the sister finished with a small smile. 'Have you a home, a family you can go to in England?'

'You mean you're kicking me out of Chuanga?' Samantha's voice was light, almost jovial. 'And I thought I was indispensable.'

'Come on, Sam!' The sister shook her head. 'You have a baby to consider. You know you can't stay. We've already discussed that. You were already making plans to leave us...weren't you?'

'Yes.' Samantha closed her eyes. If the truth were known she hadn't really got around to the point of making plans; she had been too busy thinking about her husband, about the fact that he didn't want their baby.

'You...you haven't told anyone that I'm pregnant, have you?' she asked suddenly, her eyes flicking open anxiously.

'Just your doctor... I'll have to fill in a report for headquarters, though, Sam.'

That was to be expected, but even so her heart sank.

'Shall I make some enquiries about getting you back to civilisation?' the sister asked gently now.

'I suppose you should.' Samantha nodded. 'As you say, I can't stay here.'

She watched as the sister walked away across the ward. At least her baby was all right, she told herself positively.

Ben—had he been here—would probably have been disappointed by that news.

Across the ward she could see Josh leaning indolently against the doorway, listening intently to something Joanne was telling him.

He was very handsome. His very presence seemed to dominate the small ward, radiating powerful, vital waves of strength.

What was Joanne talking so earnestly to him about? Samantha wondered. Josh seemed very interested, his eyes serious, watching her with complete absorption.

She sighed and turned on her side, away from them. She was grateful to Josh for rescuing her but she still didn't like him. He was too arrogantly sure of himself. He was probably a womaniser into the bargain. A man who enjoyed breaking hearts.

Ben had broken her heart. She stared at the wall and tried not to think about her husband. There was no point in analysing their relationship any further. If the truth were known their marriage had been a terrible mistake from the beginning. She had tried very hard to make it work, but Ben had killed her feelings for him with his cold, almost indifferent attitude.

She remembered his reaction when she had told him she was pregnant. 'Get rid of it,' he had said stonily, with no hesitation. The memory made her shudder.

Ben was dead, and she grieved for the tragic waste of his life. But her respect for him had gone. Now her priority was her unborn child.

CHAPTER TWO

A WEEK later they let Samantha out of hospital. In one way she was relieved to be out of the ward. It had been frustrating to have to lie there when she knew the nurses around her could use some help. However, going back to the room she had shared with Ben would be hard.

She was making her way out of the hospital when she saw Josh Hamilton walking towards her.

'Almost didn't recognise you with your clothes on.' He grinned as he stopped beside her. 'I've only ever seen you in a uniform or a white nightshirt.'

Samantha tried not to look embarrassed by the remark, or by the way his eyes were assessing her in a light-hearted manner. She was wearing a cotton summer dress which had a faded floral print in blues and pinks. It was not a sophisticated dress but it was pretty, or rather it had looked pretty before she had lost so much weight. Now it hung on her slender frame in a way that was not exactly flattering. Not that she cared about her looks, and she certainly didn't give a damn what Josh Hamilton thought of her.

'I thought you might have left by now,' she said crisply, pointedly ignoring his remarks.

'If you can't drive, getting out of here is not so easy,' he said, indicating his wrist, which was still bandaged. 'Believe me, I've explored all the options.'

'I know what you mean.' Samantha nodded. 'I was

hoping to be able to catch a plane to Salanga, but unfortunately none of the air relief has been able to get in.'

She turned to continue walking and he fell into step beside her. 'You're leaving?' He sounded surprised.

'Yes... I've been given my orders to go home. Apparently I need peace and quiet so as to heal my emotionally traumatised body.' She made a joke of the subject, her lips curved in a smile that didn't quite reach her eyes. 'What about you? Are you going back to England?'

'No, I'm not due to leave Nuangar for a while yet.'

They walked out into the heat of the day. The sky was a perfect dazzling blue which contrasted sharply against the brown mud huts and the dusty red earth. People were going about their work as usual. The sound of children's singing drifted up from the school at the far end of the compound.

The hospital was the only brick building among a collection of mud huts huddled together at the edge of the African bush. Chuanga had once been a thriving little community, but since the war conditions had become unbearable. They were surrounded by hostile terrain, where the warring factions allowed very little to come in or out. Except for the radio, they were cut off from the outside world.

It was early afternoon, and quiet for once. She realised suddenly that the gunfire had stopped. The calm, tranquil sound of silence was like a blessed balm to her stretched nerves.

'It amazes me how the people of Chuanga seem to remain so cheerful, even under the worst of conditions,' Josh remarked idly.

'Yes, I know,' Samantha agreed. 'I used to wander down to the school sometimes and talk to some of the children who had lost their parents. When I heard about some of the hardships they have had to endure before getting here, it made me think my own childhood was paradise. People in the West forget how well off they are sometimes... We tend to take things for granted.'

'I presume you are talking about little things—like food, running water and medical aid?' Josh enquired, raking a hand through the thickness of his hair and grinning. 'Let me assure you that I will never take a juicy steak, a hot shower or a beautiful nurse for granted again.'

Samantha felt her cheeks growing pink at the seductive, drawling words. 'Being out here certainly changes your perspective on things,' she agreed, injecting a prim, disapproving note in her voice.

'It does indeed.' He watched as she came to a halt beside a large thatched rondavel—the name given to the mud huts which served as living quarters.

There was a look of uncertainty on her face as she paused by the door, then she looked up at him. 'Well, it was nice talking to you, Mr Hamilton,' she said briskly.

'Josh,' he corrected her quietly, his eyes never leaving the pallor of her skin, the darkness of her eyes. 'I feel we know each other well enough to leave formalities behind...don't you?'

'Well...' She struggled for some polite answer, but could find none. The truth was that she didn't want to drop formalities where this man was concerned. For some reason she wanted to keep every single barrier she possessed well and truly in position.

'Can you drive, Samantha?' he asked suddenly.

She frowned, flicking her hair out of her eyes to look up at him with curiosity. 'Well...yes... Why do you ask?'

'Open that door, invite me in and I'll tell you,' he said firmly.

She hesitated. Part of her wanted to invite him inside, but she didn't want to give this man the wrong idea...she didn't want him to think she might be interested in him, because she certainly wasn't.

'I'm not going to take advantage of you,' he drawled impatiently. 'For one thing you're not my type...for another I might look like a chauvinistic, insensitive brute but I'm not really. It's a disguise I've had to adopt over the years.'

'You've certainly perfected the technique,' she said archly, wondering whether to be angered by his words or amused by them. Then curiosity overtook caution. 'Well, you had better come in, then.' She opened the door and led the way into the room.

It was stark inside—just a bed covered with a mosquito net, a rough-hewn table and a small cupboard. The only decoration was two photographs on the table. Josh glanced around at the spartan furnishings, his eyes lingering for a moment on the photographs. One was of her parents; it was faded, and in black and white, but it was the only reminder she had of the parents she had barely known. Next to it was her wedding photograph, with Ben smiling down at her in a tender way.

Samantha pulled out the one and only chair by the table. 'Make yourself comfortable,' she invited a trifle self-consciously. She noticed with gratitude that some kind person had left some soft drinks for her in a cool-box by the bed.

She picked up a bottle and held it out towards him. 'Would you like a drink?'

'I don't suppose you have a cold beer in there?'

'I'm a nurse, not a magician,' she said stiffly.

He grinned at her look of disapproval. 'An orange juice, or whatever it is, would be great—thanks.'

She took the tops off the bottles and handed him one. 'I'm afraid I haven't got any glasses.'

'Beggars can't be choosers.' He held up the bottle in a salute before taking a long, thirsty drink.

For a second she found herself watching him curiously. He looked incongruous in the small chair. He was very tall, very powerfully built, with wide shoulders tapering to lithe hips. His long legs were stretched out in front of him in a manner that suggested he was very relaxed, yet Samantha sensed that for all his laid-back manner he was taking in his surroundings with a trained, observant eye. Perhaps a keen journalist never relaxed and always noticed everything.

He was looking again at her wedding photograph, and Samantha's nerves stretched painfully as she followed his gaze. She sat down on the side of the bed.

'How long were you and Ben married?'

'Nearly two years.' Her voice was stilted.

'Strange.' Josh shook his head. 'I saw his parents when I was in London last October. They never mentioned anything about you.'

For the briefest moment Samantha hesitated. She and Ben had met through their work in Chuanga and had married there. She had only met Edward and Sarah Walker once, when she and Ben had been granted leave after their wedding to go back to England for two weeks.

'They didn't approve of the match.' She was proud of the way she kept her voice so cool, and her expression didn't falter. The hurt and the disappointment she had experienced where Ben's family were concerned was buried deep.

'Why ever not?' He frowned.

'Something to do with the fact that I wasn't Helen.'

'Ah...' His voice trailed off knowingly.

'You knew her?' Samantha's interest was immediately piqued. She had heard so much about the beautiful, clever Helen Roland from Ben's mother that it had been embarrassing—especially as Ben had never before mentioned the woman's name to her. Afterwards, when Samantha had questioned him about Helen, he had been infuriatingly vague, saying she was just an old girlfriend.

'Yes, I knew her,' Josh replied.

'You are quite close to the Walker family, then?' For some reason she had thought that Josh was merely an acquaintance.

'I saw a lot of them as I was growing up. Ben's father and mine were partners in a law firm.'

'So you know how much Sarah thought of Helen?'

'Oh, yes.' Josh nodded, his manner relaxed. 'Helen was a medical student, very clever. Ben went out with her for three years and Sarah took it very much for granted that they would get married. But then I suppose you know all the details?'

'Not really.' Samantha shrugged and met Josh's steady gaze. She wondered what he would say if she told him that Ben had married her on the rebound...that he had still been in love with Helen Roland.

Not that it mattered any more. She sighed. 'Poor Sarah. She will be absolutely devastated. It will be especially hard for her as Ben was an only child.'

For a moment a picture of Ben rose in her mind. Medium build, sandy blond hair. She took a deep breath. He had been so badly injured in the bomb blast that he had been virtually unidentifiable.

'He was a good doctor.' She looked up at Josh, unaware of the deep sadness in her eyes. It was awful, but it was the one complimentary thing she could think of to say about him. 'Very dedicated to his work.'

'That's something I would have thought you both had in common,' Josh answered gently as he put his drink down on the table. 'Will you come back to work in Chuanga, Sam, after your enforced rest?'

'I...I don't know.' She shrugged vaguely. She couldn't tell him that it would be impossible for her to return. She couldn't bring herself even to mention that she was pregnant.

'I suppose it might be considered a waste of a good nurse if you don't?' he ventured casually.

'Probably, but there are other worthwhile posts.' Samantha's voice was brittle. That theory of Josh's was certainly one her husband had favoured. He had been horrified when she had suggested giving up her career for her baby.

Her eyes clashed directly with Josh's watchful gaze. 'So why did you ask if I could drive?' She went straight to the point before he could start asking any more questions about her life and about Ben. She felt Josh Hamilton wasn't the reticent type when it came to asking questions, but then she supposed that went with the type of job he did. He obviously wasn't afraid to talk to her about Ben—unlike Samantha's colleagues, who had all skirted around the subject in a nervous way for fear of upsetting her.

'Because it suddenly struck me that I have a Jeep outside but can't drive it and that you can drive but have no form of transport.' He spread his hands. 'The sensible thing would be for us to pool our resources, don't you think?'

'You mean that I should drive you back through the bush to Salanga?' She sounded as surprised as she felt.

'Why not?' He shrugged. 'Don't you think you could do it?'

'Of course I could do it.' Her reply was instant, and then she hesitated. 'But isn't it very dangerous to drive through the bush without some form of protective escort?'

'It's very dangerous to stay here,' he pointed out laconically. 'Either way you're taking a calculated risk.'

That much was true. At one time, Samantha wouldn't

have hesitated. She had never lacked courage and had never been frightened to take a chance, but that had been before she had found out she was pregnant. Now she had to consider the risks, weigh up the danger she would face with regard to her child. 'I'll have to think about it,' she said cautiously.

He looked surprised. 'I would have thought it the ideal solution. You know that even catching a plane out of here has a risk attached to it.'

'Yes, I realise that,' she muttered impatiently. 'But I can't leave immediately anyway. There's a memorial service the day after tomorrow for Ben.'

'Well, we could leave the day after that.' He shrugged. 'I can drive some of the way,' he continued blithely. 'It's only certain sections of road that I would need you to take the wheel.'

'How long would it take?' she ventured cautiously.

'Anything up to forty-eight hours.' He shrugged again. 'Depends on conditions.'

'You mean it depends if there is a land-mine on the road…or an ambush.'

'You could get shot just crossing over towards the hospital,' Josh pointed out grimly. 'Your husband didn't even leave the hospital.'

He watched the shadows flickering across her expressive face. 'I didn't mean to upset you,' he said more gently. 'I just wanted to point out that danger surrounds us here every day.'

'Obviously I realise that,' she told him stiffly.

'I know the road between here and Salanga and I think our chances for making it through are pretty high.' He went on as if she hadn't spoken. 'Otherwise I wouldn't have suggested it.'

'Well, I'll still have to think about it.'

'Because you're frightened of being alone with me, or frightened of being out in the bush?'

'I'm not afraid of you.' Her cheeks flushed with annoyance at the suggestion. 'But I want to weigh up the dangers and think sensibly about it, that's all.'

'Fair enough.' For a moment his eyes moved over the long length of her dark hair and then the delicate curve of her face in a way that made her heart suddenly miss a beat.

Suddenly she found herself wondering if she was after all just a little bit afraid of being out in the wilds alone with such a man.

'I will look after you, Sam. You're Ben's widow and I have enough respect for an old friend not to take advantage of the situation.'

'That's apart from my not being your type, I suppose?' she said drily.

He laughed at that. 'There's no need to sound quite so disappointed.'

'Don't be ridiculous!' For a moment she was outraged. What was it with this man? Did he think that every women he met was attracted to him?'

He got to his feet, his manner insouciant. 'You are allowed to laugh, you know…even when you are in mourning. Sometimes it even helps.'

'Say something funny and I'll oblige.' She glared at him, her eyes bright with dislike. The man was damned infuriating. 'And I wouldn't bother trying to convince me that your arrogant manner is just a front either,' she couldn't help tossing in for good measure. 'Because I don't believe a word of it.'

To her annoyance he seemed to find her words amusing. 'Well, you can take comfort from the fact that it will be better to be out in the wilds of the bush with an arrogant chauvinist than a timid wimp,' he said with a grin as he turned for the door. 'You know where I am when you make up your mind.'

She was left alone then, her eyes glaring into the back of the door as it closed behind him. She didn't like Josh Hamilton, she told herself for the hundredth time. The thought of spending forty-eight hours driving alone through the bush with him was not a pleasant prospect.

She got up and put her drink down on the table. Then her eyes moved to the photographs beside her and she took a long, shuddering breath.

She had to get out of here—away from the memories of the lie she had been living with Ben. Back to safety and a new life, for her sake...for her baby's sake. In that moment she knew she would accept Josh's offer. The alternative, of staying here in this room, was too bleak to contemplate.

CHAPTER THREE

THE iridescent pearly light of dawn was streaking the African sky as Josh and Samantha loaded the truck for their journey.

The morning air was fresh and still cool. Samantha shivered slightly as she watched Josh putting a first-aid kit and large water and petrol cans safely in the Jeep. She pulled her cardigan closer around her slender figure, glad that she had decided to wear lightweight jeans for this journey—a journey that was making her feel more nervous by the minute.

She felt she had made a momentous decision in deciding to travel with Josh. She just hoped it wasn't a decision she would have cause to regret.

Josh leaned into the car and opened the glove compartment. A cool flicker of light reflected on the cold steel of a hand-gun for just a moment before he closed the door on it again.

'We don't need that...surely?' she asked breathlessly.

'Probably not.' He shrugged, then, turning, met her wide, horrified stare with calm eyes. 'I don't intend to use it.'

'Then why have it?'

'Because it might mean the difference between life and death,' he said in a cursory tone. 'Sometimes it pays to have a deterrent, something that will buy you time.'

Samantha wasn't convinced; that much showed on her

expressive face. Josh bent to pick up the suitcase that was sitting on the ground next to her and changed the subject.

'Is this all you're taking?' he asked as he tossed the small case into the back of the Jeep.

'That's it.' She shrugged a trifle self-consciously. 'You don't tend to collect a lot of belongings living out here.'

He smiled at that. 'My ex-wife never travelled anywhere without three large suitcases—two for her clothes, the other for her fashion accessories.'

Samantha digested this piece of information silently. Josh was divorced…or rather he had been divorced…maybe he had remarried by now. It struck her at that moment that she knew very little about this man—a man she would be entrusting her life to for two days out in the middle of nowhere. She swallowed down the apprehensive thoughts.

Josh had been a friend of Ben's; he must be all right. Besides, if it hadn't been for Josh she would probably not be alive today, she told herself rationally. 'Was your ex-wife a fashion model?' she asked drily after a moment.

'As a matter of fact, she was.' He grinned at her.

Samantha wasn't sure whether he was teasing her or not. 'Well, she certainly wasn't a nurse at Chuanga Hospital,' she said with a shrug. 'The only accessories you can lay your hands on here are bandages, and we're fast running out of them.'

He laughed at that and slammed the back of the car shut. 'On that happy note, perhaps we should hit the road and get out of here now?'

She nodded, her heart starting to beat a rapid, nervous tattoo again. It wasn't just the thought of the danger that lay ahead of them on the road that made her nervous, it was the thought that she was leaving her job, the place that had been her home for over two years, and she was leaving to face an unknown destiny.

A door opened behind them and Sister Roberts came out with Nurse Kelly and several of Samantha's work colleagues.

'We thought we would give you a royal send-off.' Joanne Kelly grinned at Samantha. 'We're going to miss you.'

'Not too much, I hope,' Samantha said honestly, her gaze moving to the sister anxiously. 'I must admit that I feel incredibly guilty about this—as if I'm running out on you, that I'm letting you down by leaving.'

Sister Roberts shook her head. 'You're a fine nurse, Samantha and you have worked well for us over the years. We are grateful for that.'

The two women embraced. 'Take care,' the sister whispered as they pulled apart.

When Samantha turned to get into the Jeep she saw Joanne reaching to kiss Josh full on the lips. 'Good luck,' she was saying softly. 'And if you ever come back this way, look me up.'

Samantha swung herself up behind the wheel. 'When you are ready, Mr Hamilton,' she said as she started the engine.

He grinned at that, but didn't exactly hurry himself. 'Thanks for looking after me so well, Joanne,' he said, touching the nurse's face with a gentle hand.

Samantha revved the engine and he turned and got in beside her. 'What's the matter, Sam?' he asked derisively. 'Anybody would think you were jealous.'

Irritation flitted briefly through Samantha as she put her foot down on the accelerator. 'Of what?' she grated sardonically. 'You do like to flatter yourself, don't you?'

He laughed at that, his laugh warm and attractive in the early-morning air.

Then she turned to wave to her colleagues and her irritation with Josh Hamilton was forgotten. She drove slowly out of the hospital compound, past the church where just a couple of days ago she had said a final goodbye to her husband, then down the narrow village street. A few schoolchildren standing along the roadside waved to them happily and shouted goodbye, their faces bright and smiling, their clothes shabby but well washed. Their laughing, playful voices drifted in the early-morning stillness.

As they left the village of Chuanga the sun was lifting higher in the sky, turning it from gold to crimson. Ahead the road was straight and undulating through the scrubland. Even though it was still early, heat shimmered against the horizon, like a molten wave of water.

The road was uneven and they bounced against the suspension as Samantha crunched through the gears.

Josh grimaced. 'You may as well keep the Jeep in top,' he advised drily. 'You don't have to worry about traffic lights or junctions, just a few wild animals who might decide to cross your path.'

She pushed her long hair back from her face and flicked him an impatient look. 'I'm not completely stupid,' she told him brusquely.

'I hope not,' he said laconically. 'Otherwise I would never have asked you to drive.' He picked up a pair of binoculars and trained them on the road ahead for a moment.

He's so arrogant, she thought angrily. Joanne must be completely off her rocker to find such a man attractive.

Then the surface of the road changed to what amounted to a mere dirt track. 'Keep your foot down,' he directed her curtly as they hit the rough patch and she instinctively started to ease up on the gas.

'Who is driving this car?' Her tone was sarcastic.

'You are.' He grinned at her, his eyes moving over the

soft curves of her body. 'And may I say you are doing so beautifully?'

'Don't patronise me,' she told him crossly. Then she found the car wheels spinning ineffectually as they became momentarily stuck in deep ruts in the road.

'I hate to say, I told you so,' Josh drawled. 'But if you don't keep your foot down that's going to happen again and again.'

'Did anyone ever tell you that you're a know-it-all?'

'I've been called worse.'

Gritting her teeth, she did as he said and the vehicle jerked along obligingly. As they drove, it felt as if the car was walking over the terrain, first one side then the other, negotiating small hillocks and deep gouges in the earth.

As the hours passed and the sun climbed higher in the sky the heat became more and more intense. Dust flying in through the open top of the Jeep caught on Samantha's throat until it felt like sandpaper.

'It's like an oven out here,' she commented rawly, unfastening the top buttons on her T-shirt in a vain attempt to let some cool air flood over her body.

Josh glanced at his watch. 'Nearly midday,' he murmured almost to himself. 'We haven't done bad.'

'Thanks.' She cast a sardonic glance in his direction at the grudging compliment. *She* was the one who 'hadn't done bad'.

Josh grinned, leaned over into the back of the Jeep and brought out a can of cola. 'Can I tempt you to something refreshing?'

Samantha's eyebrows shot up in surprise. 'Where did you get that?'

'Corner shop,' he answered drolly.

She frowned. 'You know what I mean. Cans of that particular drink are like gold-dust these days in Chuanga.'

'Strange how the most ordinary, mundane things assume enormous desirability when you can't get them, isn't it?' He smiled. 'This was a parting gift from Joanne. She really is quite a girl.' He held the can out to her.

Was there an innuendo in those words somewhere? she wondered grimly. Did he mean that his laid-back, devil-may-care indifference was what made Joanne so keen...or was the heat making her read things into an innocent remark? Despite the fact that her throat felt parched and on fire, she had a moment of hesitation before accepting the drink. Something about Joanne Kelly's blantant desire for this man irritated her immensely.

'Are you referring, in your own modest way, to the fact that Joanne found you attractive?' she murmured caustically as she tipped the can to her lips. The liquid wasn't as cold as she would have liked it, but it was nectar to her parched throat.

A gleam of amusement lit his eyes. 'Well, actually, I would never describe myself as ordinary or mundane, but...' He shrugged. 'As they say, beauty is in the eye of the beholder.'

'Yes, there's no accounting for taste.' She handed the can back to him. 'Do women usually throw themselves at you like that?'

'Only on days with a Y in them,' he said with a mischievous glint in his green eyes.

'Very funny.' She turned her attention firmly back to the road in front of them. 'What does your wife think about it?' she asked nonchalantly.

'She's my ex-wife. I thought I'd already mentioned that fact.'

'I'm surprised you haven't married again, what with all these women chasing you.' Samantha's mouth slanted in a wry smile.

'The idea doesn't appeal,' he said, lifting his binoculars

and scanning the horizon again. 'Some men just aren't cut
out for marriage.'

Was he like Ben? she wondered suddenly.

'Want me to take over while you get something to eat?'
Josh's voice brought her attention winging back with a
jolt.

'Are you up to driving?' she asked hesitantly.

'I'll manage. The road is pretty good here.'

If Josh described this road as good, she wasn't looking
forward to the bad bits. Driving here had been like driving
across a motorbike assault course.

She pulled the Jeep to a halt and got out to change
places with him. It felt good to stretch her legs; she hadn't
realised just how stiff she had got behind that wheel.

The air was hot and still, and a few grazing impala
nearby turned to watch them warily, ready for flight at the
first sign of danger.

'It's so beautiful out here,' Samantha sighed as she settled herself in the passenger seat. 'Hard to believe that
there is so much fighting.'

'Hard to believe man's stupidity, you mean?' Josh
eased the Jeep forward again, his voice grim.

His tone of voice startled Samantha. 'You sound angry.'

'You bet I'm bloody angry, but what good does it do?'
He was silent for a moment. 'All I can do is report on the
atrocities I see and hope that a small seed of sanity will
grow.'

The words surprised Samantha. She hadn't pegged Josh
Hamilton as the type who gave a damn. Suddenly she
found herself wondering if that assessment had been un-
justly harsh. 'My experience of your colleagues has led
me to believe that most reporters here are only interested
in getting a sensational story,' she murmured lightly.

'Not wishing to sound rude, but you don't strike me as

the type of person to be experienced in very much except for what goes on at Chuanga Hospital,' he quipped tersely. For a second he took his eyes off the road to let his gaze rake over the pallor of her skin, the soft, vulnerable slant of her mouth.

'Like life and death, you mean?' Her eyes shimmered frostily. 'Mr Hamilton, I've lived in the middle of a civil war for over two years. Take my word for it when I say that I've learnt a few things along the way.'

'I'm sure you have, but it hasn't toughened you up, has it?'

She frowned. 'I'm not sure I understand the significance of that question. Have you got to be tough to be worldly-wise?'

He shrugged nonchalantly. 'Put it this way—you don't look very streetwise. There's something about you that suggests softness, vulnerability. You look as if you need looking after.'

Samantha was totally outraged at those words. 'I can look after myself.' Her voice shook slightly with the force of her emotion. 'I can assure you that I'm a past master at it.'

He cast a speculative glance at her. 'So Ben wasn't the protective type?'

She looked away from him out towards the vast empty plains. 'I didn't get married to have a protector.'

'No, of course not.' His voice was cool and steady. 'Why did you get married?'

Her head turned swiftly, her eyes cutting into his with furious intent. How had they managed to skate onto the thin ice of the subject of her marriage? She was damned if she was going to discuss such personal matters with a complete stranger. 'The usual reasons.' She bit the words out sharply. 'Not that it's any of your business.'

'Of course not.' He sounded totally unperturbed by her anger.

For a moment there was silence, and she thought that the conversation was at an end. Her heart was beating uncomfortably hard against her ribs.

'By "usual reasons" I presume you are talking about love?' he said after a minute or two, flicking those cool green eyes over her once more.

'For heaven's sake!' she flared heatedly. 'Of course I mean love!' She swallowed hard, trying desperately to quell the rush of emotion flooding through her. She would rather die than admit to Josh Hamilton that Ben had never loved her, that their marriage had been a hollow sham. She had her pride. 'You knew Ben. Do you think he would have married someone he didn't love?' She glared at him with the full force of her feelings.

Josh shrugged. 'I suppose not.' Then his voice changed and became surprisingly gentle as he met the shimmer in her eyes. 'I'm sorry, Sam...I didn't mean to upset you. That was crass of me.'

'Doesn't matter.' Her voice was brittle as for a moment she had to fight against the tears that wanted to fall.

Conversation stopped for a while. Then Josh said kindly, 'I put the food in the cooler unit behind you; why don't you help yourself to something?'

The last thing she felt like doing was eating. 'Maybe a little later.' She leaned her head back against the car seat, trying to appear nonchalant, trying to hide the fact that her emotions were racing around in circles. 'I'll just rest for a while,' she said lightly, and closed her eyes against the glare of the sun.

Inside, her mind was whirling around and around over Josh's words. 'Why did you get married?' 'Usual reasons...usual reasons...' The words played over and over like a parody in her head. What would Josh have said if she had turned around and told him the truth—that she had married out of a desperate need for warmth and affection? He would probably have found that terribly amusing.

She opened her eyes, and to her embarrassment found her gaze colliding with his.

'Aren't you hungry?' he asked gently. 'You should really eat something.'

'I suppose so.' Her voice was unenthusiastic. It was only the thought of her baby that made her reach into the back to comply.

She held out some of the meagre rations to him but he shook his head. 'You go ahead; I'll have something later.'

Samantha ate mechanically, her eyes fixed on the far horizon. A herd of zebra caught her attention as they ran across the plains, their black and white stripes made hazy by the dancing heat so that they seemed to merge with the landscape as if they were a growing part of it. Slowly she started to relax.

She shouldn't really have snapped at Josh the way she had, she thought with contrition. Since she had become pregnant her emotions had seemed to see-saw dramatically, making her feel things acutely. These days she was never quite sure if her feelings could be trusted or if they were merely distorted by hormones. Sometimes she wondered if this whole episode in her life was merely a bad dream...one that she would wake up from at any minute.

She glanced back at Josh. He was a tough-looking man, his features etched in a hard-boned face, his jaw square and determined. There was nothing dream-like about him; he was a rugged, vital male from the tip of his unruly dark head of hair down over his lithe, well-toned body. Dominant was the word that sprang to mind as she looked at him. Dominant and powerful—a man who was always in charge of a situation, who invariably got what he wanted.

Why had he got married? she wondered idly. Had he been wildly in love? For some reason she suspected that with Josh Hamilton there would be no half-feelings. He was the type of man to feel something totally.

'Feel better now?' he asked, turning to meet her eyes.

She nodded. 'Sorry if I was a bit sharp before,' she said huskily.

'Don't worry about it. It was my fault anyway. I guess asking awkward questions is one of those idiosyncrasies that a reporter never loses—even when he isn't working.'

'Well, let's just forget it anyway,' she said brightly, then changed the subject. 'Would you like me to take over the driving again?'

'I thought you would never ask,' he said with a laugh.

After that they travelled in a companionable silence. The road wound higher as they reached the mountainous region of Charracana. At one point the dirt track was just wide enough for one car, and the drop on the left-hand side of the Jeep was sheer, giving dizzying glimpses of the dry river basin hundreds of feet below.

'I'm glad this isn't a busy thoroughfare,' Samantha joked nervously as she negotiated the twists in the road with extreme care.

'I'm just glad you're a competent driver,' Josh said with a gleam of humour in his voice. 'Because I'm the one staring down at the drop.'

When the road dipped into the valley on the other side the sun was starting to go down in a blazing ball of violent orange. Josh suggested that they pull the car off the road and call it a night.

'The road is worse a little further on,' he said seriously. 'I think we need to negotiate it in daylight.'

Samantha nodded. She had no wish to travel along

roads like these in the dark. 'Where do you think we should stop?'

He pointed ahead towards where the undergrowth was thicker. 'Up by the trees. Pull it well off the road—that way it will be hidden if anything happens to pass in the night.'

A shiver of apprehension darted through Samantha at those words. She knew very well that he was referring to rebel guerilla forces. They were in very dangerous territory now. No man's land.

As soon as she had pulled the Jeep to a halt, Josh got out and started to gather pieces of branches and greenery to drape over the bonnet of the vehicle.

'May as well minimise the risk of being seen,' he said as she got out to help him. 'That way we can sleep a little easier.'

By the time the sun had gone down the Jeep was festooned with branches and leaves.

'Pretty good handiwork,' Josh remarked as he stood further back on the road to survey their efforts. 'Shall we break out the dinner rations before putting our heads down?'

Samantha nodded and then glanced around at the dark undergrowth that surrounded them. 'I'm going to have to pay a visit to the little girls' room first.'

He grinned and held out a torch towards her. 'Better take this and watch out for snakes. We have all the mod cons out here.'

Her heart skipped a beat at the thought. 'I think I've just gone off the idea.'

'Go on.' He waved her towards the bushes and then added jokingly, 'Don't be long or your dinner will be ruined.'

'Well, we can always reheat it in the microwave,' she said, joining in the spirit of things as she turned away.

Her smile faded a little as she moved carefully into the lush vegetation behind her. The thought of snakes and God knew what else made her decide not to go too far. She was back to the relative safety of the car in a few seconds.

At first she couldn't see Josh, just the vague, camouflaged shape of the Jeep. Then he peered up over the branches. 'I decided to book a table for two in here,' he said cheerfully. 'Can you climb in so as not to disturb our handiwork?'

'I might just manage that.' It took her a moment to hoist herself up and then swing her legs over the door. 'Don't leave the waiter a tip,' she panted as she slid into her seat. 'Damn bad table he's given us.'

'Good view of the conservatory, though.' Josh handed her the dry biscuits that had become part of their staple diet at Chuanga since the supply trucks hadn't been getting through.

'Definitely no tip for the waiter,' Samantha said as she bit into one. 'The food here is terrible.'

'I can't understand it—I ordered us both a steak,' Josh said with a shake of his head. 'And, believe it or not, this place came highly recommended.'

'Who by? Kermit the Frog?' Samantha smiled.

'Actually it was Fozzie Bear.' Josh crunched into another biscuit and washed it down with water. 'Hell, these are awful. Soon as we get back to civilisation I'm going to treat you to a good meal.'

'Is that a promise?'

For a moment their eyes met and held.

Why had she said that? she wondered, her heart jumping nervously.

'I believe it is.' He reached out a hand and touched her cheek. It was a curiously tender gesture and it sent a shiver racing through her.

'Of course, the offer is subject to availability,' he said, moving away from her again.

Then Samantha just smiled. He was joking, of course. When they got back to civilisation they would just say goodbye and their ways would part for ever.

She leaned her head back to look up at the sky, her dark hair falling away from her face, leaving its youthful, classical features exposed to the silvery moonlight.

The night was incredibly beautiful—the stars were big and bright and clear, and the moon looked almost like a piece of costume jewellery, sparkling and too large to be real.

For a moment she found herself remembering how she had looked out at the sky the night of the mortar attack on the hospital. She had wondered that night which direction she should take next...what to do about Ben's rejection of their baby.

It seemed that fate had decided those things for her. One direct hit on the hospital and her life had veered sharply on a path for home, in the company of a stranger she barely knew.

Who decided these things...? Had Ben's death been written down in some book up in heaven? Was her fate written there too? She shivered at that thought. Of course her fate wasn't written; life was what you made it. She remembered her mother saying that to her many years ago.

'Are you cold?' Josh reached into the back of the Jeep and pulled out one of the blankets to throw it over her legs. 'The nights are colder up in the mountains.'

'Thanks.' Her voice held the edge of a tremor.

'Eat up,' he urged gently. 'The management have sent a good dessert to make up for the main course.' He held up a squashed chocolate bar.

She laughed. 'You are full of surprises, Mr Hamilton.'

'The surprise is that it hasn't melted completely. At least the cold night air is good for something.'

Samantha smiled. She liked the way Josh could turn a dreadful meal, a dangerous situation into something light-hearted. She was about to reply when he suddenly moved, and his hand clamped firmly down over her mouth.

A wave of surprise flooded through her. If this was Josh's idea of a joke she didn't think it at all funny. She was about to struggle, make her discomfort and annoyance at such an action clear, when Josh whispered for her to be quiet in a tone that held no hint of a joke.

Cold fear trickled down her spine in that moment as she heard what he must have heard seconds before her: the distant sounds of voices.

Her eyes, wide and horrified, met his as those voices came closer and she recognised the native dialect of one of the fiercest warring tribes.

She knew that if they were found now, their time was up.

CHAPTER FOUR

HER breath froze inside her and her heart slammed against her chest as the voices came nearer.

Josh took his hand from her mouth and pulled her down towards the floor, his finger going to her lips in a caution to keep absolutely silent. He needn't have worried; Samantha couldn't have made a sound even if he had wanted her to.

Petrified, she could only stare at Josh's face as they crouched together on the floor. The voices stopped and for a moment there was just the sound of the insects in the undergrowth. Samantha hadn't realised before what a racket they made; the noise filled her eardrums as she strained to hear any movement from the people outside.

The sound of a match striking nearby made her heart leap wildly. It sounded as if someone was standing right next to the Jeep.

There was a low murmur of voices again.

Samantha didn't think she had ever been as frightened. Her hand moved instinctively towards her stomach, her thoughts for a moment veering to her baby. All sorts of weird thoughts spun around her mind in a terrifying couple of seconds. Then the voices seemed to move away from them just a little.

Josh moved back from her with the stealth of a cat and cautiously climbed a little way up on the seat to risk a look over the branches that had hidden them. He dropped back beside her a second later and came close to whisper against her ear.

'Just six of them.'

His voice was so low that she had to strain every muscle to hear.

'Looks like they're going to make camp here.'

Samantha's eyes widened. If the group stayed until morning they would definitely be found. The Jeep's camouflage might work at night, but as soon as daylight broke she felt sure they would be easily spotted.

He saw the panic in her eyes, the nervous pulse that beat in her throat, and he reached out a hand to stroke the smooth curve of her cheek in an instinctively reassuring gesture. 'We'll be all right.' Then he pulled her in close against the warmth of his body and held her tightly.

She didn't try to pull back from him. Strangely, the close human contact was just what she needed at this moment. It was reassuring, comforting. She buried her head against him, listening like a frightened animal for any sounds outside. The only sound that she could hear was the steady beat of Josh Hamilton's heart.

How long they stayed like that she didn't know; it felt like hours, but it could have been minutes. When Josh pulled away from her she felt cold, bereft. She watched as he chanced looking out over the top of the door again.

'They're asleep,' he whispered as he sank back down to her.

'What will we do?' Her voice was faint.

'Try and do likewise.' He smiled at her look of consternation. 'Don't worry. I'll keep watch on the situation.' He glanced at his watch. 'Approximately seven hours to dawn. We'll stay put for six hours; if they are still here then we'll leave.'

'Leave the Jeep?'

'We'll have no choice. As soon as the sun comes up they'll see it.'

Samantha swallowed hard.

'Come on, try and get some sleep.' He reached for the blanket that was lying beside them and put it carefully around her. 'Use my knee as a pillow.'

'I can't sleep,' she hissed softly.

'Try.' He put a hand at her back and pushed her firmly down towards him. 'It's important, Sam,' he whispered urgently. 'You'll need all your strength if we have to walk tomorrow.'

She hesitated for a moment and then did as he asked, curling down beside him and putting her head on his lap. It wasn't very comfortable, and she was sure she would never sleep, but she closed her eyes to please him.

An animal howled in the distance, its cry unearthly, like a soul in torment. Samantha huddled closer to Josh. His arms went around her, his hand stroking the silky softness of her hair. For what seemed like a very long time she was tense and frightened, listening to every sound outside with bated breath. Josh continued to stroke her hair. The touch of his hand was soothingly hypnotic, and after a while she felt her heartbeats slowing, felt her eyes beginning to close as exhaustion started to overtake her best efforts to keep awake.

When she next opened her eyes daylight filtered down on her through the leafy branches draped over the Jeep. She was alone in the vehicle and fear rushed back as she remembered last night and the danger that had surrounded them. Where was Josh? She sat up cautiously, her heart slamming against her chest, and abruptly a wave of nausea swept over her.

She swallowed hard on the awful feeling. Morning sickness was something she had been plagued with since the beginning of her pregnancy. Desperately she fought against it; she couldn't afford to be ill now.

Josh was standing next to a camp fire, his hands on his hips as he stared down at a pan boiling on it. He turned sharply as she moved.

'Well, good morning.' His face lit with a smile as he saw her. Then his eyes narrowed on the deathly pallor of her skin.

'Are you OK?'

'Yes...yes, fine.' Thankfully the feeling was starting to subside. Perhaps it wasn't morning sickness, just apprehension and nerves. 'What happened?'

'Well, there are two pieces of good news and one bad,' he said easily.

She started to relax at his laid-back manner. Relief was heady, like a good wine running through her body. Josh was smiling, so nothing could be that bad. 'What are they?' She pushed her hair back from her face, feeling groggy and only half-awake, but gratefully not ill.

'Our neighbours left about two hours ago, and they were heading back the way we have come so we don't need to worry about bumping into them again.'

'Thank heavens for that.' Her voice was fervent. 'What's the bad news?'

'There's no bacon and eggs on the menu.' His teeth flashed white against his tanned skin. 'Will black coffee suffice?'

The mere thought made Samantha's stomach protest. 'I think I'd just like some water, please,' she said, trying to push at the branches against the door of the Jeep to get out.

He came across to help her. As he opened the door he held out his hand to assist her in climbing out. It was fortunate that he did because she stumbled as she tried to move, her limbs stiff from the cramped position she had slept in.

His arms were strong as they caught her, and for a moment she allowed herself to lean against him. Then she bent to rub her legs.

'Pins and needles?' He didn't let go of her immediately.

She nodded. 'Must have been the way I was lying.'

Josh laughed and bent to rub her legs with brisk movements. For a moment she was just relieved by the firm massage as he made the pain start to subside. Then she became aware of the touch of his hands in a different way—a way that made her heart stop beating for a second. Abruptly she pulled away from him. 'That's fine now,' she told him crisply.

He straightened and looked at her. For a moment there was a tension between them that she didn't dare to examine too closely.

'I'll get you some water.' He moved away from her towards the fire.

She watched as he lifted the canister and carefully poured her a cup.

'Come on.' He looked round at her as she just stood watching him. 'If I put this down on the ground the ants will drink it before you get a chance to even sip it.'

She tried to smile and moved closer to accept the plastic cup he held out towards her. Carefully she avoided looking at him as she did so. Had Josh noticed how she had just reacted to the touch of his hands? She cringed with embarrassment as she thought about the charged silence of a moment ago. Of course he had noticed. Josh Hamilton didn't miss anything.

Her senses reeled. She was shocked by the flare of desire that had started to uncurl inside her at the touch of his hands. No...it wasn't desire, she told herself forcefully. She just wasn't awake properly. If Josh imagined otherwise that was his mistake.

'Would you like a biscuit or some fruit?' Josh sat down next to a rucksack that he had taken from the back of the Jeep.

'No, I'm not hungry, thanks.' She watched as he helped himself to a piece of fruit from the bag. On second thoughts, maybe he hadn't noticed anything, she told herself as she started to feel a bit better. Knowing Josh, he would have made some sarcastic comment if he had.

He looked remarkably fresh, considering the way they had spent the night. His dark hair sat smoothly back from his face; his denim jeans and shirt were not even slightly creased. The only thing different about him was the dark stubble on his face, but strangely that just seemed to enhance his dark good looks even further. She had to admit grudgingly that she could see why Joanne Kelly had been so smitten with him. He was very attractive.

He glanced up and caught her watching him, and she looked quickly away.

'How long before we reach Salanga?' she asked, trying to appear nonchalant, trying to rid herself of the strange thoughts travelling around her head.

'We should arrive at dusk, if all goes well.' His eyes travelled over her thoughtfully. 'Do you feel up to driving?'

'Of course.' She put a self-conscious hand to her hair. In contrast to him, she felt an utter wreck. Her T-shirt was creased. Her hair felt wild. But it didn't matter what she looked like, she told herself furiously; she wasn't interested in gaining admiring looks from Josh Hamilton.

Slowly she sipped her water and moved closer to the fire, glad of its warming effect. A cool morning mist enshrouded the valley. The sun's rays were watery as yet, sending orange and yellow shafts of light dancing on the mist. The only sounds were the crackle of the fire and the calls of birds.

'I thought we were going to die last night,' she said suddenly. 'If those tribesmen had found us...' She shook her head, unable to form the words to describe what they might have done.

'But they didn't.' Josh's voice was calm. 'Forget about it now.'

She put down her cup and nodded. He was right. They had to go on fearlessly; there was no point in dwelling on what might have happened or what might happen. Even so the thought of the journey ahead seemed even more frightening today than it had done yesterday—maybe because they had come so near to death.

She took a deep breath. 'Is there enough water for me to wash my face before we go?'

Josh picked up the canister and handed it to her. 'Go easy on it.'

She felt much better after she had freshened up. Then she bent her head and rigorously pulled a brush through her long hair, so that it fell back in vigorously restored luxuriant waves. As she straightened she caught Josh watching her and that feeling jolted through her again. This time there was no mistaking it for anything but blatant sexual awareness. Her heart hammered against her chest viciously. She was horrified with herself and totally shocked.

'We should be going.' Josh turned and kicked over the traces of their fire. 'Are you ready?'

'Whenever you are.' Her voice sounded strained even to her own ears.

He moved to pull the branches away from the Jeep. 'We should travel as far as we can before the heat starts to get intense.'

Silently she moved to help him.

'You OK?'

'Fine.' She didn't dare meet his eyes. She was still trying to wrestle with the strange emotions he had just aroused in her with just a look.

'You're still very pale.'

She was too aware of him, of the disturbing intensity of his eyes.

'I probably need more sun.' From somewhere she found the strength to joke.

He smiled at that. 'Actually, I didn't think it was possible for someone with such a lightly tanned beautiful skin to look so pale.' He reached out a hand to touch her face, but she moved abruptly away from him before he could make contact, her heart thumping wildly.

'I hope you're not trying to flirt with me.' Her voice was stiff and angry. But the anger was directed as much at herself as at him. She couldn't believe that she was allowing him to affect her in this way. 'Do I need to remind you that my husband has only just died—that you were supposed to be a friend of his?'

'You don't need to remind me of anything.' His voice was very cool now. 'And I wouldn't dream of flirting with you. I'm sure I'd get a warmer response from those tribesmen last night.'

She threw him a dark, fulminating glare. 'Shall we go?' she said icily.

'Oh, I think we should.' He put the water canister back in the Jeep. 'The sooner we get to civilisation the sooner we can get out of each other's hair.'

As they set off the sun's golden rays started to warm the chill of the day. It did nothing, however, to thaw the atmosphere in the Jeep. Neither spoke as the vehicle bounced over the rough terrain of the valley and then started to climb up the mountain road on the other side.

Josh had been right when he'd said that this piece of

road was worse than the one before. It was so steep that Samantha had to keep the Jeep in low gear all the time. The engine strained against the steep, slippery slope, making her decidedly apprehensive—especially when she noticed the drop down at the side of her.

As they climbed higher and higher Samantha started to feel more and more apprehensive. Her hands felt clammy against the steering wheel, her breathing was shallow and uncomfortable. 'You didn't say the road was this bad.' She shot him an accusing look as the vehicle rounded a corner that would have been more suited to a mountain goat than a four-wheel drive.

'I'm sure I did.' Josh's voice was very relaxed. 'You're doing very well.'

Somehow the soothing tone aggravated her nerves.

'I'm not doing very well at all.' She cast a look down at the drop next to her and felt the backs of her legs go weak.

'Don't look down.' A warning note crept into the clipped command. 'It's not far before we reach the top, and then the road twists along the narrow pass before it drops down.'

'You should have warned me about this.' She bit down on her lower lip. She'd known she hated heights, but she hadn't realised just how much she hated them until now. She felt slightly dizzy, and her cotton T-shirt was sticking to the soft curves of her body.

When they reached the top the road levelled out for a while and Samantha took the opportunity to stop the car.

It felt as if the world about her was spinning in a wild blur of blue sky and red dust.

'Come on, Sam, don't cave in on me now. You've done really well.'

Josh's smooth voice penetrated the mists, and suddenly they started to clear in one almighty angry wave.

'How dare you subject me to this?' She rounded on him, her eyes blazing, her breath catching in sharp waves. 'That road was terrifying. You should have prepared me...you should have said something.'

'If I'd said something you wouldn't have driven up.' His manner was still calm, almost insouciant.

'Damn right I wouldn't.'

'Sam, you've done it.' He reached out to put a hand on her shoulder.

She shook him off. 'No, I haven't. We've still got to get down.' She reached for the doorhandle, intending to step out of the vehicle in an attempt to pull herself together.

'Sam, don't—' Josh tried to stop her but he wasn't quick enough, and the door swung open.

It was a big mistake. She turned and found herself sitting looking down a narrow gorge that plunged for several hundred feet. The road was just about wide enough for her to get out, but she would have had to edge sideways along the car.

For a moment she was shocked into silence.

Josh reached across her and closed the door, and the action seemed to release her from the paralysis which gripped her.

'I've got to get out of here.' She hoisted herself up in the seat and made to climb across him to get out on his side, near the face of the mountain. She couldn't think straight. All she could think was that she wanted to be away from the edge of that cliff.

'Samantha, stop it.' He grabbed her forcefully around the waist and pushed her back down. He was very strong but she struggled against him in a kind of wild frenzy.

'Let me out.' She pummelled wildly against his chest, then tried ineffectually to push him out of her way.

'Stop it!' It was then that he shook her sharply. He

didn't hurt her, it was more a small jolt, but it silenced her effectively. She stared up at him, reproach eloquent in her wide eyes.

Then to her horror she felt tears welling up inside her.

'Come on, Samantha.' He reached over and folded her in against him. 'The worst is over now.'

She couldn't answer him; she was fighting the weakness inside. She wouldn't cry. She couldn't break down in front of Josh—especially over something like this. She was made of tougher stuff.

She took a deep, shuddering breath and pressed her face closer against his chest. 'I...I think I'm afraid of heights.' She muttered the words incoherently into the light cotton shirt. She could feel his skin through its fine material, firm and tightly muscled.

'I think it's probably a bit more than that. It's more likely that you're suffering from delayed reaction. Sister Roberts did say—'

'What did she say?' She pulled back from him, instantly on the defensive.

'That you had been through a lot...that you needed looking after.' He smiled gently, teasingly at her. 'I put her mind at rest and volunteered for the job.'

'I've told you already that I can look after myself.' Her voice was angry. She sincerely hoped that the sister hadn't told him about her pregnancy. Her heart thudded unsteadily. No, she wouldn't have done that; she had promised not to.

She stared ahead at the terrifying narrow pass with its hairpin curves and horrifying drops down to a deep gorge, and a tremor raced through her.

'Would you like me to take over the driving for a while?'

She darted a nervous glance at his hand. She knew it

would take complete precision to steer a safe course around here. 'Are you up to it?'

He laughed at that. 'Well, I'll give it my best shot. I don't particularly relish the thought of going over the edge.'

She thought about it for a moment, then shook her head. 'No, I'll be all right.'

'I know you can do it.' His voice was warm with encouragement—a fact that Samantha was very grateful for. His faith in her gave her a renewed boost of courage and gently she eased the vehicle forward.

It took several hours to get around the cliff face. On a few occasions Josh had to get out of the Jeep and direct her forward, to make sure that the wheels were not going over the edge.

She heaved a sigh of relief as they started to make their descent.

'Please tell me that the worst of the roads is now behind us,' she demanded forcefully as the road levelled out. 'I couldn't bear to do anything like that again.'

'That's the worst over with,' he said obligingly.

She pulled the car to a halt and flicked a disbelieving glance at him. 'Really?'

'Really.' Then suddenly he reached across and kissed her cheek. 'You were wonderful.'

She was already hot, but the touch of his lips against her skin raised her temperature even higher. She stared at him, eyes wide, wondering why he had done that. 'I don't feel very wonderful,' she told him curtly, trying to ignore the strange feelings the touch of his lips had set up inside her. 'In fact I feel pretty awful. My eyes hurt from staring into the sun, my throat's dry and I'm so hot that I feel as if I'm cooking.'

He put his hand against her cheek in a way that sent her blood pressure soaring. 'You are hot.'

She moistened her lips nervously. His eyes followed the movement of her tongue. Her heart thumped unmercifully hard against her chest. She could feel the sun's rays pumping down on them, cruel, unrelenting. The heat was so intense that it was almost unbearable.

She wrenched her eyes away from him and forced herself to think clearly. 'I'd like a drink.' Her voice sounded raw and unsteady. Her eyes scanned the road and she noticed a lone tree up ahead. 'Shall I pull into the shade for a moment?'

'Good idea.' He sounded perfectly normal, and she wondered if she had imagined the feeling of tension between them a moment ago. Perhaps the heat was getting to her.

It was a relief to reach the shade. She switched the engine off with a sigh. 'I'd give anything for a shower.'

'Well, it won't be long now.' Josh pulled the rucksack out of the back and poured two cups of water. 'I reckon we'll make Salanga by dusk. There's a hotel with hot and cold running water down by the airport strip. It's not luxury but it's not bad.'

For a moment Samantha was silent. They were very nearly at the end of their journey, and when they reached Salanga they would go their separate ways. She might never see Josh Hamilton again. That fact shouldn't have bothered her, but strangely it did. Although she had been frightened whilst she had been on the road and there had been times when Josh had really annoyed her, a feeling of comradeship had also grown between them.

She glanced over at him and their eyes met and held.

'What plans have you made for when you reach England?' he asked suddenly.

She shrugged. 'Rent a flat in London, I suppose.'

She hadn't allowed herself to think too far in advance. She had some savings—enough to see her through until her baby was born anyway. 'I'll look around for another job,' she murmured reflectively, almost to herself.

He frowned at that. 'You're definitely not coming back to Chuanga?'

'No.' She sipped her drink, her eyes lowering over the expressive spark of anxiety that lit her eyes.

'I can't say I blame you,' he said gently. 'You've been through enough out here.'

She made no reply to that. For a moment she wanted to tell him that she was pregnant and that that was her sole reason for leaving. The words refused to be spoken.

'Have you got family in London?' he asked curiously.

'An aunt who lives in Chelsea.' She finished her drink and handed her cup back to him. 'Are there any biscuits left?' She changed the subject suddenly. 'I'm starving.'

He rooted through the bag and brought out a couple. 'Well, that's one good thing,' he continued smoothly, as if the interruption hadn't occurred. 'London can be a lonely place.'

Samantha's lips twisted. Yes, it was a lonely place. She knew that from experience. And when she got back she would be on her own; she couldn't expect too much from her aunt...she was a busy woman with her own career. She didn't want to think about it. One day at a time was as much as she could focus on.

'Do you get on with your aunt?' Josh probed suddenly, his eyes perceptive as they took in the different expressions on her face.

She smiled. 'You've got your reporter's hat on again,' she remarked sardonically. 'But, yes, I do get on with Sylvia. She took me in when my parents were killed in a car accident. I don't think she particularly knew very much about children.' A wistful smile crossed Samantha's face for a moment. 'I was rather a shock to her. A plain, skinny ten-year-old didn't fit in very well with her glamorous lifestyle. She's a singer, and she travels around a lot.'

'So did you travel around with her?' Josh asked curiously.

Samantha shook her head. 'I couldn't. There was my schooling, and I had to be in London for medical reasons... I was in the car accident that killed my parents, you see.' Her voice softened for a moment as painful memories crowded down on her. 'I had years of physiotherapy and quite a few operations before I was pronounced well again.'

'How awful. Who did you live with during that time?'

'Mostly Aunt Sylvia, but when she was working away I stayed with a foster-family.' Samantha looked away from him.

That time had been difficult. She had missed her parents so much, and the horror of the accident had lived vividly in her mind for years. She had been so relieved when the treatment at hospital had come to an end—so relieved that it hadn't seemed to matter too much when the doctors had told her she would never be able to have children. But then, at the tender age of thirteen such a thing hadn't seemed too important. It was only as she'd got older that she'd understood just how grave that statement had been.

Her hand moved instinctively to her stomach. Sometimes she still couldn't believe what a miracle it was that she was pregnant. Her eyes swam hazily with tears at the joy, and then with sadness as she remembered Ben's reaction. She had never seen him so angry. He had furiously accused her of deliberately tricking him and trying to wreck his career.

When she had started dating Ben she had told him honestly that the doctors had told her she could never have children. When he had still gone ahead and asked her to marry him she had believed that he accepted her situation and loved her regardless of whether she could have children or not. It had never occurred to her that his whole attraction to her had been based on the fact that he thought they would never have a family. Ben had wanted a working partner, not a wife.

'I can't believe your aunt didn't give up her travels to look after you.' Josh's voice cut into her thoughts. 'It was a bit hard of her to leave you with foster-parents...wasn't it?'

'Not really.' Samantha honestly didn't blame her aunt for following her career. 'Sylvia had a dream of becoming a great singing star. She was entitled to chase her dream.'

'I guess you're right,' he conceded gloomily. Then abruptly he changed the subject. 'So what's your ambition, Sam?'

She shrugged. 'Just to be happy, I guess,' she said truthfully.

'What's happiness?' he asked steadily. 'A lot of money? Another job in nursing?'

She looked up and met his direct gaze. 'Getting to Salanga would make me pretty happy,' she said with a grin. 'Should we move on now, do you think?'

His lips curved in a lazy, teasing smile—a smile she was getting very used to. 'I guess that's my cue to stop asking nosy questions?'

'I guess it is,' she admitted huskily. 'To be honest, Josh, I don't know what I want. The future is not something I'm at all certain of right now.'

'Who is?' he said with a shake of his head. 'What's the old saying? Life is what happens to us while we're making other plans.'

She smiled sadly.

For a moment his gaze rested on the softness of her lips, the large, melting blue eyes. He seemed about to say something, and then he leaned forward and his lips touched hers.

For a moment she was so surprised that she sat absolutely still, her heart dipping down into her stomach and back again as if she were on a merry-go-round. Thinking about it later, she felt sure Josh had only meant to kiss her lightly, perhaps in a brotherly fashion. Yet when their lips met something very strange happened.

An instant chemistry flared inside her, and after the initial shock she found herself responding in a manner that could only have been described as hungry.

His unshaven skin was abrasive against the softness of hers, yet for some reason that only seemed to add fuel to the erotic sensations he was arousing inside her.

His lips were passionate, warm. She moaned incoherently—a small sound in the base of her throat that spoke of desire and need. Almost in response his lips became more demanding, ravaging against hers in a way that sent bittersweet arousal sweeping through her body.

All she could hear was the sound of her heart. All she could think about was the fact that no one had ever kissed her like this…had ever made her feel like this.

Instinctively she tried to move closer, her body arching, straining to be next to his. Her breasts pressed against his chest. She could feel the heat of his skin burning through the thin material of their clothes and her nipples hardened instinctively.

She wanted him to touch her; she wanted it so badly that even through her haze of desire she was shocked.

He was the one to take control of the situation. His hands caught her upper arms and gently he pushed her back.

Her breathing was uneven and out of control, as if she had been running a race. She stared up at him, her eyes wide with burning passion, then consternation as reality hit her.

'I'm sorry, Samantha.' He shook his head. 'That shouldn't have happened.' His voice held only a slight uneven edge.

Shame sizzled in the aftermath of desire. She had thrown herself at him. She couldn't believe that she had behaved so badly.

'Damn right it shouldn't.' Her voice trembled.

The silence between them was the most uncomfortable, the most unnerving she could ever remember.

'Samantha, we're both overwrought, the heat is adding to the craziness of the situation and—'

'Stop it.' She cut across him in a blazing tone. She felt humiliated enough without his running through a list of excuses. In all honesty she couldn't get too angry with him. It had mostly been her fault. She acknowledged the truth silently. He had probably been totally surprised by her response.

She darted a glance up at him and remembered him telling her in no uncertain terms that she wasn't his type. 'It was all my fault.' She spoke in a tightly controlled voice. 'I…I'm the one who's sorry.'

The lean, handsome features didn't give much away; there was no flicker of emotion in the deep eyes. 'I don't think it was all one-sided.'

Lord, he was going to be all gentlemanly about it. Her eyes flickered closed as she strove to get control of the situation and salvage some sense of pride and decency. 'Look, I've just lost my husband—I wasn't trying to…to come on to you. I'm just—'

'I don't think we need to go quite so deeply into this.' He stopped her abruptly, his voice stony. 'It was just a kiss. Let's just agree to forget it, shall we?'

She nodded, but didn't dare to look at him.

'We should be hitting the road again.' His tone was brisk and businesslike. 'I suggest you slide over here and I'll take the wheel for a while.'

Samantha did as he asked. Her heart was beating in a very strange manner and she had a ridiculous feeling of disappointment. What on earth was the matter with her? she wondered bleakly. What had she expected Josh to say? There was nothing to say.

Heat waves shimmered in front of them as Josh pulled the Jeep back out onto the road. Samantha, feeling the sun's fiery rays being absorbed through her dark hair, reached into the back of the car for her wide-brimmed rather battered straw hat. Then she leaned back against the seat.

She tried very hard not to think about that kiss, about the desire he had set alight so easily. It was far too disturbing.

They didn't speak for a long time, and as the minutes ticked by Samantha felt a sad sense of loss stealing deeper and deeper inside her. She couldn't understand the feeling; she was utterly confused, utterly dejected.

When she couldn't bear the quietness any longer she chanced a glance across at him. He looked stern, his eyes studying the road ahead intently, his mouth set in a firm, unequivocal line. She tried not to think about how that mouth had felt against hers. That wasn't being sensible; that was foolish in the extreme.

'What are your plans once we reach Salanga?' she heard herself ask steadily.

'A shower and a cold beer.' He didn't take his eyes off the road.

She smiled lightly. 'What, no steak?'

He looked at her then, and she felt a frizzle of electricity as she met those eyes. His lips curved in his lazy, attractive smile. 'Salanga is civilised compared to Chuanga. But it's not *that* civilised.'

'Well, it's all new to me. I was flown directly into Chuanga from Zaire.' She was conscious of a sense of relief at the light conversation. Yet conversely the seeds of melancholy lingered.

'You haven't missed much.'

She turned the subject lightly back to her original question. 'So, what are your plans—after the beer and the shower, of course.'

'A good night's sleep.' He shrugged. 'Then I'll leave for an assignment in the north of the country at first light tomorrow.'

Samantha swallowed hard. 'Isn't it very dangerous up there?'

He laughed at that. 'Sam, I've got news for you…it's very dangerous out *here*. Danger is part of my job.'

And he seemed to thrive on it, just as Ben had thrived on it. She only hoped that Josh would be luckier than her husband.

Samantha fell silent with the grim thoughts that whirled around in her head. Up ahead the dirt road wound through a thickly wooded valley. It was quiet and deserted, and so beautiful that it made her want to cry.

She blinked back the tears furiously. Wretched hormones, she thought angrily, then sighed and leaned her head back against the seat, watching the dark shapes of birds circling against the cloudless sky.

'Why don't you try and get a few hours' sleep?' Josh glanced across at her pale, strained features. 'You look worn out.'

She felt more than tired, she felt exhausted, but she doubted that she could sleep; there were too many things to think about.

'I'll just rest my eyes for a minute,' she said staunchly.

* * *

The next thing she knew, Josh was shaking her awake. 'We're here,' he said gently. 'Sam, we've made it.'

'Made it?' She sat up, feeling disorientated and for a moment just a little sick. Wearily she pushed her dark hair away from her face and looked about her.

They were outside a rather run-down-looking building situated at the crossroads of what looked like a sleepy one-horse kind of town.

'Salanga.' Josh leaned closer to her, his eyes raking over the pale, almost transparent appearance of her skin.

She should have felt ecstatic. Yet the only thought in her mind was that this was the parting of their paths. Salanga was goodbye as far as they were concerned.

CHAPTER FIVE

STEPPING into the hotel was like going back into the past. It had an air of faded glamour. Once it had probably been a very stylish place to stay, but now the war and time had taken their toll on the place and the decor and the furnishings were antiquated. The one thing in its favour was the overhead fans, which sent a deliciously cool waft of air down over them as they stepped across to the reception desk.

'Mr Hamilton, sir, nice to welcome you back.' The young girl behind the desk gave Josh a warm smile.

'Nice to be back.' Josh leaned nonchalantly against the desk. 'We'd like two of your best rooms, Mary.'

The girl nodded and turned to pick up two keys from the pigeonholes behind her. 'Rooms next to each other with connecting doors,' she said with a gleam in her eye. 'Will that suit?'

'Admirably.'

Josh laughed as they turned to go upstairs and he caught Samantha's look of outrage. 'The girl was only joking, Sam.'

'No, she wasn't,' Samantha hissed in a low tone. 'She thinks we are having an affair or something.'

Josh laughed even louder at that. 'Honey, if we were having an affair I would not be content with connecting doors, I can assure you.'

Her skin burnt with furious colour at that.

He flicked a glance over at her. 'At least that's succeeded in bringing some colour to your cheeks,' he said softly. He stopped by the lift. 'You go on up—' he held out her key '—I'll go and get our stuff from the Jeep.'

She waited for what seemed like ages for the lift but it never arrived. In the end she took the stairs. Thankfully her room was on the first floor—the way she was feeling she didn't think she would have had the energy to walk another step. The room was bright and airy and she noticed gratefully that it was clean.

A wave of fatigue swept over her and she went across to sit down on the edge of the bed. Lord, she had never felt as tired as she did right now. Slowly she eased her shoes off and then glanced across and caught sight of her reflection in the dressing-table mirror. She was a total mess. Her clothes were creased, her dark hair tumbled wildly about her shoulders, her face was unbelievably pale. She shuddered. No wonder Josh had asked if she was feeling well...she looked a wreck.

Resolutely she stood up and headed for the bathroom. The sight of clean white towels and soap brought a smile to her face. Heaven right now was a hot shower.

She heard Josh knocking on the bedroom door as she finished rinsing her hair. 'I'm in the shower,' she called out. 'Just leave my case by the bed.'

'Didn't take you long.' He laughed.

'The sight of my dirt-streaked face in the mirror was enough to send me running in here for cover,' she called out with a smile.

'Your face looked fine to me...a little pale, perhaps. Anyway, I deviate... What I really want to ask is will you join me for dinner tonight?'

Samantha's heart missed a beat, then she rationalised swiftly. It was just dinner—no big deal. It was obvious he would ask her to accompany him. They were in the same hotel, the same dining room—he could hardly sit across the other side of the room from her. Even so it felt strange being asked to dinner by another man. There hadn't been anyone in her life except Ben for so long.

'Sam…did you hear me?' Josh called out as she made no reply. 'I said, how about dinner tonight?'

'I heard you.' She turned off the water and wrapped her body in a large bathsheet before wrapping a smaller towel turban-style around her head. 'I'm…I'm just not sure.'

With a cursory glance in the mirror to check that she was decent, she unlocked the bathroom door.

The sun was going down now and the room was in semi-darkness. Josh was sitting on the edge of her bed, his face in shadow as he had his back towards the window.

'You look like an exotic dancer dressed like that,' he said softly, his gaze moving over the slender curves of her figure and the long length of her legs. There was an intimacy about the moment that threw Samantha's senses into chaos. She found herself thinking about the way they had kissed earlier and her heartbeats accelerated wildly. The desire, the smouldering need he had unleashed inside her, was unlike anything she had ever experienced.

'So, you were telling me why you're not sure abut dinner,' Josh continued in a jovial tone. 'Aren't you hungry?'

Surprisingly she was a little; her shower seemed to have revived her more than she had a first realised. 'Yes… but…' She trailed off, not really knowing what to say. She could hardly tell him that she was afraid of the emotions he seemed to stir up in her with such ease.

'It's just dinner, Sam,' he said patiently. 'I'm not asking you to sleep with me.'

Her face flared bright red at those words. 'No…of course not!'

He grinned. 'I'm saving that until later.'

She turned away from him. 'You're outrageous, do you know that?' She knew he was only joking, but her heart thumped unmercifully hard against her chest at the mere suggestion.

'Am I?' Amusement rippled in his tone. He got up from the bed. 'I'll make a reservation in the dining room for seven-thirty.' He glanced at his watch. 'That gives you half an hour, all right?'

She nodded wordlessly.

She was wearing a cornflower-blue dress when Josh called for her a little while later. She was aware that the colour suited her, brought out the deep unusual shade of her eyes, but she was unprepared for the way Josh seemed to do a double take at her appearance as she opened the door for him.

'You look lovely.' The warmth of his voice and the gleam of male appreciation in his eyes made her heart bounce crazily.

'Thank you.' She was aware that her voice sounded prim, but she couldn't help it.

His lips curved in a wryly amused smile. For a moment her gaze locked on those lips. They were sensual, she thought hazily. Sensual...passionate.

'Well, if you're ready, we'll go downstairs.'

'Yes, of course.' She stepped hastily into the hallway, her hair swinging in a shining wave of mahogany as she briskly closed the door behind her and fell into step beside him.

She felt angry with herself for allowing her emotions to run with such wild abandon. She had never felt so acutely conscious of a man before. It was the weirdest sensation—as if all her senses were tuned into him.

'Let's take the lift down, shall we?' He touched her

arm lightly for just a moment and she felt her skin burn from the contact.

She darted a nervous glance at him as they stepped into the close confines of the elevator.

He was cleanly shaven, and his hair, still slightly damp from the shower, looked darker somehow. He was wearing a short-sleeved white shirt which emphasised his deep tan, and a pair of faded jeans which clung to lean hips.

'You're very quiet.' He smiled across at her.

'Just tired, I guess.'

He nodded. 'It's the heat.'

Was it the heat that made her keep remembering the way he had kissed her this afternoon? Slow fingers of desire seemed to stroke inside her at the very thought of his lips against hers, the touch of his hand against her body.

She looked away from him and took a deep breath. She wished she could understand these feelings. They were so intense. She had never felt such a powerful attraction for anyone before and it was deeply disturbing to feel like this now, for someone who was, after all, just a stranger to her.

The lift doors opened with a swish and they were in the restaurant. She wasn't even his type, she reminded herself as the waiter came over to lead them across to a table. He had told her that right at the very beginning. What was his type?

Blonde and leggy with model-girl looks. The idea sprung into her mind as they sat down at a table at the far side of the room. Yes, Josh would definitely go for the model-type—after all, his ex-wife was a model.

'The menu is a bit limited.' Josh grinned across at her. 'Vegetable stew or ragout of beef.' He put down the menu card. 'I think I'd recommend the vegetable dish. God alone knows what kind of beef is in the ragout.'

Samantha grimaced. 'Thanks for the warning. I'll take the stew.'

Josh ordered the food and then ordered himself a beer. 'What about you, Sam?' he asked. 'There's no wine, but the beer isn't bad.'

She shook her head. 'Orange juice, if you have it?' she asked the waiter.

'Don't you drink?' Josh asked as the waiter retreated to get their drinks.

'Sometimes,' Samantha answered hesitantly. She did drink occasionally, but now that she was pregnant she would be abstaining.

'We don't really know very much about each other, do we?' he said suddenly. 'And yet sometimes when I look across at you I feel I've always known you.'

It was a strange kind of thing to say, but somehow Samantha knew what he meant. She glanced across at him. He had very nice eyes, she thought absently—light green with dark flecks in them. Sometimes they looked like the sea on a wild, stormy day... She caught herself up abruptly. What was wrong with her? She wasn't interested in Josh's eyes, or anything else about him for that matter.

'I suppose that's your way of saying these last couple of days have seemed like an eternity.' She forced a light, jovial note into her voice.

He laughed. 'Actually, the journey wasn't as bad as I thought. Apparently the roads further north are far worse at the moment.'

Her heart thumped painfully. 'Does that mean you won't be going north tomorrow?'

He shook his head. 'No, I'll be leaving at first light.'

'What about your arm?' she asked anxiously. 'You shouldn't really be driving yet.'

'I have a colleague going with me. She'll do the driving.'

'She?' Samantha looked across at him in surprise.

'Jenny Wright—she's a first-rate camerawoman. We've worked together on quite a few assignments.'

'I see. It's a good job you're not chauvinistic about women drivers. It seems to be your week for being chauffeured by them,' Samantha remarked a trifle drily.

'Oh, I like being driven by women,' he answered with a teasing gleam in his eyes. 'Just as long as they don't try any parallel parking.'

'Very funny.'

Their food and drinks arrived at that moment. Although the meal looked good and reasonably wholesome, Samantha's appetite had suddenly deserted her.

'Well, I suppose this is a farewell dinner,' she said lightly. 'I'll have to see about getting a plane out tomorrow.'

'I mentioned it at the desk. Mary said she would phone through to the aid agency, let them know you've arrived.'

'Thank you.' She toyed with her food. 'It will be strange being back in London again.'

'It's not such a bad place.' Josh shrugged. 'Being in a country like this makes you appreciate it all the more.'

She nodded. 'One thing's for sure—I don't think I'll ever complain about the British weather again. It will be wonderful to see the rain.'

He laughed. 'Wonderful for a few weeks, then you'll be longing for the sun.'

'I don't think so. At least I'm going back at a nice time of year—I love the spring. The cherry blossom will be out soon, and the tulips.' She sighed wistfully. 'One thing I've really missed while out in Africa is the seasons.'

She looked across and caught him watching her intently. 'What do you miss most about home?' she asked him curiously.

'My son,' he answered without hesitation. 'But then, I missed him before I left London.'

'You have a child?' She stared across at him, taken aback by this piece of information.

He reached into the back pocket of his jeans and brought out a wallet. Flipping it open, he held it across to show her a colour photograph of a young boy who had dark hair and green eyes.

'He's very like you... How old is he?'

'He was eight last December.' He put the photograph away. 'Alex spends his summer holidays and if possible Christmas with me. It's not enough. I miss him like crazy.' The words were spoken bluntly, and for a moment a fierce gleam of emotion burnt in the depths of his eyes.

'He lives with his mother, I take it?' she asked gently.

He nodded. 'Sophie left when he was four years of age—took him to live in Paris.'

'Why Paris?' Samantha frowned, a dart of sympathy flowing through her for Josh.

'She was madly in love with a French photographer.' he told her with a trace of acrimony. 'Although I have my doubts about that. I reckon half the attraction was the fact that Bernard relaunched her modelling career.'

Samantha thought she detected bitterness in that statement. Was Josh still in love with his ex-wife? The idea flitted briefly through her mind.

'Anyway, the fact that she took Alex so far away ruled out the possibility of my being even a weekend dad.' Josh shrugged. 'I filed for custody but the judge, in his infinite wisdom, decided that Alex was better off with his mother.'

'I'm sorry,' she said sincerely. 'It must have been awful for you.'

'It was a rough time—for Alex as well as for me.' Josh reached for his drink. 'But he was young and he has adjusted to the situation. Apparently he gets on well with Bernard and he speaks fluent French, so...' he shrugged '...I suppose things could be worse.'

'I suppose so.' For a moment she reflected on the difference between Josh and Ben. Ben hadn't wanted his child...Josh had gone to court to fight for his. 'If you had won custody of Alex would you have given up your job?'

'I worked mostly in London at that time, so I would have managed—with the help of childminders to bridge the gap from him getting out of school and my getting home.'

'You had it all worked out,' Samantha said lightly.

'Not enough to convince the judge.' Josh shrugged again. 'Anyway, enough of that. Why don't we talk about you? Tell me how you came to be working at Chuanga Hospital.'

It was strange how easy it was to talk to Josh. Samantha hadn't realised how fast the time was going until they were interrupted by the girl from Reception and Samantha looked up to find the restaurant had emptied.

'Sorry to disturb you.' The girl smiled pleasantly at Josh before turning to Samantha. 'Good news,' she said earnestly. 'There's a plane leaving at six-thirty tomorrow morning. They said for you to be up at the airfield about an hour before.'

She knew she should have felt delighted, yet there was a heavy weight settling over her at the thought of leaving Africa...or was it the thought of saying goodbye to Josh?

'Is there a taxi or something that can take me down there?' She kept her voice light, tried to sound pleased.

'I'll take you,' Josh offered easily. 'It's no problem.' He cut across her as she started to protest. 'Don't forget I'm leaving very early tomorrow anyway.'

How could she forget? Their eyes met and locked, and for a moment there was silence. Samantha could feel an undercurrent between them that was almost tangible. She dragged her eyes away with difficulty and glanced at her watch. 'Well, it's late. I should really turn in.'

Later, lying awake in her narrow bed, staring up into the darkness of the room, she tried to analyse the incredibly charged atmosphere that lay between her and Josh. As the parting of their ways became more and more imminent it seemed to be growing stronger, twisting between them like something alive, tugging on her heartstrings. She turned on her side and tried to tell herself that she was imagining things.

She closed her eyes and tried to sleep. She thought about her baby and a smile curved her lips. Her baby was the most important thing to her. Nothing else mattered.

She must have drifted off to sleep. A low rumbling sound made her open her eyes and for a moment she was disorientated. She thought she was back at the hospital. She thought the sound outside was the sound of mortar bombs.

A white flash of light lit the room and she sat up, her heart thudding uncomfortably hard as fear shot through her. She swung her legs out of bed and moved quickly to the window. In her haste she knocked into the bedside table and the lamp clattered to the floor with an almighty loud crash.

She stood by the window and stared out. Everything was pitch-black. The silence of the night was overwhelmingly lonely, frightening. The heat of the room was oppressive. She glanced up and found that the overhead fan had stopped working.

She wondered if the hotel had been hit by some kind of blast, if rebel forces were attacking the safe heaven of

Salanga. She moistened her lips nervously and scrabbled on the floor to find the lamp and see if the electricity was still on.

'Samantha?' Josh's soft tones from the other side of the connecting door were a welcome relief. 'Samantha, are you all right?'

Hastily she grabbed her dressing gown and crossed to open the door.

'I heard a noise outside…like an explosion—'

'There's an electrical storm raging several miles inland from here.' His voice was calm. 'It's giving quite a spectacular light show across the night sky.'

'Oh!' Now she felt incredibly foolish. She noticed he was only wearing a pair of white briefs. She tried not to look at him, her gaze moving past the naked expanse of his chest to his room. The sheets on his bed were thrown back and there was a delicious cool draught from the overhead fan.

'My fan isn't working,' she mumbled.

'I'll have a look.' He stepped past her.

Samantha watched as he tried the switch by the door. Then for a moment her eyes skimmed over him, taking in the perfect contours of his tanned body. His upper torso was powerfully muscled and dark hair curled across his chest, tapering down towards the flat line of his stomach. She veered away from him and walked into his bedroom to stand under the fan for a few moments.

'I don't know what's the matter with it.' He joined her a little while later. 'It seems to have just died.'

'I'll be—' Her words were cut off by a loud rumble of thunder. The sound made her jump.

'Thunder.' Josh put his hand on her shoulder, turning her towards the window as the night sky lit up with vivid forks of light.

He didn't take his hand away but left it resting lightly

there. Samantha could feel the warmth of his body radiating through the thin material of her dressing gown.

'You're trembling.' His hand stroked her arm in a way that was meant to be reassuring, but it made shivers of desire stroke deep inside Samantha's body. 'It's just a storm, Sam.'

It wasn't the storm outside that was affecting her, it was the one raging inside her—a storm of feeling aroused by just the touch of his hand.

She stood perfectly still, trying to fight the feelings, trying to restore some sanity to her emotionally charged body.

'Would you like a drink?' He moved away from her slightly.

She shook her head. 'I'd better get back to bed. It's only a few hours until morning.'

'You can stay in here, if you like.'

The casual offer made her heart miss a beat and she looked up at him with uncertainty, remembering how he had joked earlier about asking her to sleep with him.

'I meant that I'd take your room as the fan isn't working in there.' He grinned.

'Oh.' She looked away from him, hoping that he hadn't guessed what she had been thinking. 'Very gentlemanly of you.'

'Well, I can be urbane when it's called for.' He reached out and touched her face, tipping her chin so that she was forced to look at him. 'But what I really wanted to say was we could both share my single bed and make mad, passionate love.' His voice was suddenly very serious.

She didn't say anything. She couldn't find her voice for a moment. Her heart seemed to be in overdrive.

'But I suppose saying something like that would be totally out of order.' His hand moved from her chin, stroking away a silky strand of hair from her cheek. 'It's just that I keep thinking about the way we kissed this afternoon. I keep wondering if it was my imagination—or did you really taste so good?'

He leaned closer, his thumb moving to touch the fullness of her lips, stroking across them in a whisper-soft caress that set every nerve-ending in her body on fire.

'I was lying awake thinking about it.' His words were a murmur as he bent his head and his lips sought hers.

She felt herself leaning weakly against him as the warmth of his lips sent heat spinning through every part of her body.

Outside the roar of thunder seemed to echo the wild, clamouring need inside her. Her senses were in chaos and she leaned closer, allowing herself to reach up and touch the satin smoothness of his shoulder, then her fingers curled through the darkness of his hair.

He smelt of soap—a clean, fresh aroma that subtly invaded her senses. His lips were passionately skilled, as was the caress of his hand moving down the straight length of her back and gently positioning her so that she could feel his desire pulsing hard against her body.

His kisses were slow and deep and they seemed to invade every part of her soul. She felt his hand moving her robe aside and she murmured softly, but it was a sound of desire, a sound of need as his gently stroking fingers moved over the soft fullness of her breast.

Her dressing gown slithered to the floor, leaving her standing naked in front of him. The overhead fan wafted cool air over the heat of her skin and gently stirred her hair as Josh picked her up and put her down on the crisp white sheets of his bed.

The room was filled with a white-gold shaft of light as lightning lit the darkness for a second. It highlighted Josh's powerful body as he removed his only item of clothing and joined her in the small bed.

The feel of his naked body next to hers was the most erotic pleasure. He kissed the soft curve of her neck, sweeping her hair back as he followed the line of her shoulders. The exquisite tenderness of his lovemaking was unlike anything she had ever experienced. He was so slowly sensuous, taking time to pleasure each little part of her, whispering soft, husky endearments about how beautiful she was.

Then suddenly he stopped.

He swore softly and sat back on the edge of the bed, raking an unsteady hand through the thick darkness of his hair as he looked down at her.

'You just called me Ben.'

She stared up at him. She had been so lost in the beauty of his kisses, his caresses that she hadn't been aware of speaking. She had certainly not been thinking about Ben.

He looked away from her. 'This isn't the most sensible thing, is it? You're missing your husband and I'm taking advantage of the situation.' He stood up and reached for his clothes. Then without a backward glance he was gone.

Samantha pulled the sheet over her trembling body. She was filled with an unbearable ache of unfulfilled desire. She had wanted to beg him not to stop; she had wanted to reach out and curl her arms around him, drawing him back against her. The need for him was so great that it hurt.

She burnt with shame as she remembered how easily she had allowed Josh to undress her. She had wanted him so much...still wanted him.

Why had she spoken Ben's name? Perhaps the way she had fallen so easily under Josh's spell was, as he had suggested, some kind of rebound reaction. She clung desperately to the excuse, because coming in here and falling so easily into Josh's arms...his bed...was totally out of character for her. But even at the same time as she tried to mitigate her actions she knew that her attraction to Josh, her need for him went deeper than that.

The knowledge was frightening. She was a level-headed, intelligent woman, and she wouldn't allow herself to be attracted to Josh Hamilton. Their lovemaking would have been just a pleasurable interlude to him; it would have meant nothing. In just a few hours' time they would be saying goodbye and he probably wouldn't even give her a second thought. She remembered how the nurses had flocked around him at Chuanga, vying for his attention, and anger at her own folly flooded through her.

Even though Samantha had hardly slept at all she felt wide awake. The air was hot and still and it smelt of scorched earth.

'Pity it didn't rain here last night.' John Murray of the aid agency chatted pleasantly to them as they walked across the airfield towards the light aircraft that would carry Samantha on the first leg of her journey home. 'I honestly thought it might when I heard that thunder.'

'Too much to hope for,' Josh answered easily. 'It must be what...two years since it has rained?'

Samantha was only half listening to the conversation. She felt tense and nervous around Josh. The atmosphere between them was highly charged.

It had been very embarrassing this morning when he had knocked at the door to tell her what time it was. Then they'd had to swop over rooms so that she could get dressed and pack up the few things she had taken out of her suitcase.

She hadn't dared to look at him as she had opened the door. Had swept past him, being very careful to avoid any contact with him.

She couldn't believe that he had possessed the nerve to ask her if she had slept well...as if nothing had happened

between them! From somewhere she had found the
strength and dignity to lie politely and tell him that she
had.

They had barely spoken on the brief ride to the airport.
It had been a relief when John Murray had met them and
the awkward silence had been broken, but now, as the
first rays of gold light stole through the darkness and they
stood next to the small aircraft that would carry Samantha
away, she wished perversely that John Murray would melt
away and that they could be alone.

She listened as John said he had been in the north of
the country a few weeks ago. 'It was bad,' he said grimly.
'I was lucky to get out in one piece, and by all accounts
it's even worse now.'

She shivered at the thought of Josh going there. Suddenly the awkwardness of last night didn't seem to matter
at all. She wanted to fold herself into Josh's arms and tell
him not to go up there; she wanted to beg him to get on
this plane and come with her out of this God-forsaken
place.

'Samantha!' A voice calling across the field made them
all turn. Samantha was surprised to see Harry Unwin
heading across towards them. Tall and good-looking,
Harry was an important man in the aid agency. He had
been the one who had interviewed her in London what
seemed like a lifetime ago. She had seen him a few times
since then. He travelled extensively between London and
Nuangar, keeping tabs where he could on the exact situation in each area where they had people.

'I'm glad I caught you before you left.' He enveloped
Samantha in a bear-like hug. 'I was so sorry to hear about
Ben. You must be devastated…absolutely devastated.'

Aware of Josh watching her, she tried not to think about
last night, about how she had inadvertently murmured
Ben's name. What would Josh be thinking? That he had

been right to say what he had to her…right to stop making love to her?

'Do you know Josh Hamilton?' Hastily she tried to change the subject and introduce the two men.

'Yes, we've met before.' It was Josh who answered, his voice distant, as if his mind was elsewhere.

Harry turned and shook Josh's hand warmly. 'We got radio contact with Chuanga yesterday. Sister Roberts told me you were looking after Sam for us…it was good of you.'

'No big deal. Actually, we looked after each other,' Josh said calmly, then his eyes met Samantha's. 'I'd do it all over again, given the chance.'

It was impossible to ignore her flare of feeling at those words. Was he referring to last night? She wanted to go into his arms—she wanted to so badly that it hurt. These emotions couldn't just be due to her feeling vulnerable. They were far too strong, she thought dazedly. She had never felt like this before.

It took all her will-power to tear her eyes away from him and look at Harry as he spoke to her.

'If you need anything—anything at all—get in touch with me,' he was saying. He pushed a slip of paper into her hand. 'My home number's on there as well as my private line at the office. I'll be back in London next week.'

'Thanks, Harry.' Her voice was husky.

For a moment there was silence. She glanced at Josh and was consumed with the irrational desire for him to ask her not to leave.

Harry cleared his throat loudly, and she looked back at him as he said suddenly, 'Sister Roberts told me about the baby, Samantha. But if you need a job we're always looking for people of your calibre in the office. Your knowledge of Nuangar and the problems here would be invaluable.'

Samantha felt herself going very hot at the mention of her pregnancy. Her heart seemed to pound in her ears. She wasn't surprised that Harry knew she was pregnant— Sister Roberts had told her she would be reporting the exact circumstances behind her leaving to head office— but that he should mention it now...in front of Josh! She could sense Josh's sudden stillness, feel his eyes burning into her.

Harry glanced at his watch. 'I'd better not detain you any longer. I've got your aunt's address, so I'll be in touch. Meanwhile, have a safe journey.'

She watched as John Murray took her case on board the plane and Harry went to talk to the pilot. She was left alone with Josh.

'Why didn't you tell me?'

The quietly spoken question made her pulses race.

She turned to look at him and she didn't pretend to misunderstand. She could have said that it was none of his business, or she could have made some light-hearted remark. Instead she said softly, 'Would it have made a difference?'

His lips twisted in that attractive rugged smile she had come to know so well. 'I'd have been a hell of a lot gentler last night.'

She felt her cheeks glow with heat. 'You were gentle.' Her voice was a husky rasp of sound.

He reached out and touched the side of her face in a curiously tender gesture. The light caress sent memories of the passion they had shared flaring through her. She ached to go into his arms.

'I'm sorry if I upset you last night, Sam. I realise that you're vulnerable...distraught. I shouldn't—'

'Don't, Josh.' She shook her head. She didn't want him

to apologise. Perhaps it would be easier to let him believe that last night had been a result of her fragile emotions, that she had been kissing him but thinking of Ben, but it wasn't true. She looked at him steadily, her eyes moving over the handsome features, drinking in every detail and storing it away. Last night had meant much more...

She heard John Murray coming down from the plane. 'Ready when you are, Samantha,' he said lightly.

Josh reached into the pocket of his jeans and took out a letter. 'Do me a favour, will you, Sam? Post this. It's for Alex. I like to keep in contact all the time, and with going up north today I don't know when I'll next get a chance to send it.'

She knew that unspoken behind those words was the knowledge that he might not come back from the north of Nuangar at all. The warmth of his love for his son and the letter pressed into her hand made her eyes suddenly mist with tears.

'You will take care?' Her voice sounded strained, the glimmer of emotion barely suppressed.

'Goes without saying.' He stroked a silky strand of her hair back from her face. 'You take care of that baby—it's a precious gift to be cherished.'

Then he moved back and she felt cold suddenly... bereft.

'See you around, honey.'

With a casual wave of his hand he strode towards his Jeep—a tall, handsome stranger silhouetted against the blood-red of the morning sky.

She wanted to run after him...she wanted to hurl herself towards him and shout for him to stop.

Instead she turned silently and climbed into the plane.

CHAPTER SIX

SAMANTHA felt drained as she finished her work for the day. She had been back in London for five weeks now, and although she liked her new job at the aid agency there were days like today when she wondered if she had done the right thing in accepting Harry Unwin's offer.

Every time some news about Nuangar came in she felt her heart constricting with fear in case it was bad news about Josh. Today, when she had heard that two Westerners had been killed, she had felt sick with panic that one might have been him.

'Still here?' Harry put his head around his office door, his eyes skimming across the empty desks towards where she sat at her computer terminal. 'You're always last out of here.'

Samantha smiled wanly at that. 'No, Harry, *you* are always the last person to leave.' She admired Harry Unwin tremendously. He was dedicated to his work...and a very caring man.

'Only because I've got nothing better to do.' He grinned at her. 'Of course you could always remedy that and take me for a pizza.'

Samantha shook her head regretfully. 'I'm sorry, Harry, but I'm too tired to do anything tonight. I'm going to go home and have a bath and an early night.'

'I'll take a rain-check,' he said easily. 'By the way, I know you haven't made up your mind about what you want to do careerwise after the baby is born, but a few of the girls are going on a computer course soon—would you be interested in joining them?'

Samantha smiled at that. 'Are you telling me I need it?' The question was asked teasingly, and with the confident knowledge that she had been handling herself very efficiently over these last few weeks—a fact that still surprised her. Samantha had been very unsure about accepting Harry's offer of work, because her office skills were basic, as was her knowledge of computers. She had told Harry this in no uncertain terms but he had still insisted she would be perfect in here. He had been proved right.

'I'm not telling you any such thing and you know it,' he said now with a shake of his head.

She laughed. 'Even so…an update on the computer might be a good idea. It certainly wouldn't hurt.'

'I'll get the details together for you tomorrow.' He glanced at his watch. 'Tell you what, I'll give you a lift home—I've done enough here for one day anyway.'

Samantha accepted the offer gratefully.

It should have taken about twenty minutes to drive to Samantha's flat, but the rush-hour traffic was bad and it was three-quarters of an hour before he pulled the car into her road.

'It's here on the right.' She pointed towards a large Victorian house.

'Doesn't look bad.' Harry bent his head to look up at the building. 'I thought you said the place was basic.'

'It is inside.'

'Well, anything you need, you only have to ask. I'm a dab hand with a paintbrush, you know.'

She grinned at that. 'In between reorganising the office and flying back and forward between here and Nuangar?'

'Well, sure, I'm a bit busy—'

'Understatement of the year.' Samantha smiled. 'But it was a sweet offer, Harry. Thank you.'

'It's worth it just to see you smile.' He looked at her seriously. 'You look so sad sometimes, Sam.'

'I'm fine, really,' she assured him briskly.

'Sure?'

She nodded, wondering what he would say if he knew that a lot of the time her thoughts were on Josh, worrying about his safety.

'I'm glad, because you're a valued member of the team,' Harry said softly, then to her surprise he reached across and kissed her cheek.

'I hope you're not trying to soften me up for a pay-cut, Harry Unwin, because it won't work.' It seemed best to cover the moment with a light-hearted quip, and she was glad she had when he just laughed heartily.

'That's for next week,' he assured her. 'This week I just want you to work all the hours God sends.'

'What's new?' She laughed and reached for the door. 'Thanks for the lift, Harry.'

'See you tomorrow, then.' There was a fleeting glimpse of disappointment in his tone and suddenly Samantha realised that he had been hoping she would invite him in.

'Bright and early.' She made her voice crisp and businesslike. She didn't want any romantic entanglements—she was too busy putting her life and her emotions back together. Her baby was the only thing she wanted to concentrate on. Harry was a man she liked and respected, but that was as far as it went.

It started to rain as she got out of the car. As she turned a man getting out of a car across the street caught her attention. For a second her breath caught. He looked very like Josh Hamilton—same tall, powerful build. He was wearing a long, expensive-looking mackintosh, with the collar turned up, and his head was down against the rain. She noticed that his hair was coal-black, thick and wavy.

The memory of running her hands through Josh's hair

sprang to her mind and made an ache of longing start up inside her. She turned impatiently away. She didn't want to remember that night of madness, and of course it wasn't Josh...Josh was in Nuangar.

She wished she could stop thinking about him. Sometimes when she lay in bed at night she pictured him driving in the fierce heat of the sun. Sometimes she imagined that he had been caught in an ambush and she would toss restlessly, her heart thudding with panic for him. Sometimes she pictured him with Jenny, the camerawoman he had spoken of... Jenny was always blonde and beautiful—the model type.

The rain started to get heavy and she hurried in the front gate towards the house, scrabbling frantically in her handbag for her keys at the same time. She almost tripped on one of the steps up to the front door and a firm hand steadied her.

Samantha looked up and wondered if she was hallucinating. The man in the raincoat was indeed Josh Hamilton! She was so stunned that she couldn't say anything; she just stood staring up at him.

He reached out a hand as a raindrop caught in the thickness of her eyelashes and lightly brushed it away as it rolled down the smooth pallor of her skin.

The warmth of his touch against the coolness of her skin made her tremble, made her remember the ecstasy of lying in his arms. 'You're back.' Her voice didn't sound as if it belonged to her.

He grinned. 'Looks like it.'

All right, so she knew it had been a ridiculous statement, but she was just so overwhelmed by emotion at seeing him like this.

'Are you going to invite me in, or are you planning for us to just stand out here catching up on all the rain we missed while we were in Africa?' he asked drolly.

Same Josh Hamilton. Same infuriating sarcastic remarks...same gorgeous eyes that made her want to melt.

She hoped he didn't notice how her hand trembled as she put the key in the lock.

'So what are you doing here?' she managed to ask when they stood inside the hallway.

'Aren't you pleased to see me?' he asked lightly.

That question opened up all kinds of dangerous avenues. She decided not to go down any of them, but said instead, 'I'm just so surprised.'

'I take it Harry Unwin didn't tell you that I phoned the agency this morning?'

'No. He never mentioned it.' She turned to lead the way upstairs to her flat. 'It must have slipped his mind.'

'He said you were too busy to speak to me. I had a hell of a job extracting your address from him.'

'Well, I suppose he doesn't like giving out addresses to just anybody.'

'Unwin knows damn well who I am,' Josh reminded her abruptly. 'He's well aware that we drove together across Nuangar.'

He looked around her flat with interest as they stepped into the living room. It was small and the decor was plain, but Samantha had brightened it up with colourful scatter cushions on the settee and a woven rug in an Aztec design in front of the Adam-style fireplace. A huge vase of long-stemmed yellow roses sat on the mantelpiece.

'Nice place,' Josh commented.

'Well, it suits me for now.'

His eyes lingered on the roses. 'I suppose they're from Unwin?'

The question startled her. She had bought the flowers herself, in an attempt to brighten the room and cheer herself up.

He held up a hand before she could answer. 'Sorry, it's

none of my business. It's just that the fellow was very offhand with me on the phone. He had an almost proprietorial attitude about you.'

She shook her head, totally nonplussed by this. 'I think you're mistaken. It was a difficult day today. Emotions were running high—'

'Emotions certainly looked as if they might be running high in the car a few moments ago,' Josh commented sardonically.

She frowned. 'Were you spying on us?' At the same time as she was speaking she felt herself growing hot with embarrassment. Had he witnessed that kiss and gained the wrong idea?

'I'm a journalist, not James Bond.' He laughed. 'And I can assure you that I've got more important things to think about than whether or not you're having an affair with Harry Unwin.'

'Suddenly it's all coming back to me,' she muttered darkly.

'What is?'

'The reason I first thought of you as intensely infuriating.'

'Because I don't care who you're having an affair with?' One eyebrow lifted mockingly.

'Because you're so damn arrogant.'

He smiled, and his eyes moved over the soft, vulnerable curve of her mouth, the deep blue of her eyes. 'And you are damn beautiful...especially when you're angry.'

The compliment sent a wild shiver racing through her, but she forced herself to treat it in the light-hearted way she was sure it had been meant. 'Put away your silver tongue, Josh, because it doesn't work with me.'

'Really?' One eyebrow lifted. 'And I somehow gained the impression that you weren't exactly immune to my charms.'

The memory of how easily she had offered herself to him that night in Africa was instantly there. She turned away from him, pretending not to be bothered by the statement. 'Well, everyone is entitled to one moment of insanity in their lives.' Where she'd found the flippant tone for that answer, she didn't know. She hung her coat up and turned back to look at him with a confidence she was far from feeling.

'Is that what it was?'

The softly asked question made her self-assured manner falter. She wasn't sure why she had melted into Josh's arms the way she had. She could hardly bear to analyse it in her own mind, never mind out loud to him!

'Yes...of course. Josh, I've got a baby to think about. That is my priority. I don't want or need anything else.' She strove to sound decisive and unruffled, but her heart was thundering in her ears, almost obscuring the sound of her own voice, so she couldn't tell how she sounded.

His eyes moved over the slender curves of her figure. She was wearing a pair of stone-washed jeans that were pulled in at her tiny waist by a silver-buckled belt, and a black halter-neck top.

'You're looking fabulous.' He shook his head. 'Your pregnancy doesn't show at all. How far along are you now?'

The colour in her cheeks flared even brighter. 'Over thirteen weeks.' She moved away from him to fill the kettle and busy herself making them a drink. 'So, how long have you been back from Nuangar?' Swiftly she changed the subject.

'I got back yesterday.'

She felt quite an irrational surge of pleasure that he had looked her up so quickly.

'I wanted to ask you on the phone this morning if you'd posted that letter to Alex for me.' he said suddenly.

She nodded. 'As soon as I got back.'

'It's just that I've rung the house in Paris several times and there's no reply. I've also tried Sophie's mother's number here in London and there's no answer from that either.'

She glanced across at him. Was this why he had got in contact with her so quickly? Because he wanted to know if she had posted his letter to his son? She was aware of a twinge of disappointment. 'Maybe they're away on holiday together?'

'Probably.' He was hanging his coat next to hers. She noticed the expensive cut of his grey suit, how it accentuated the powerful sweep of his shoulders, how the white shirt emphasised the darkness of his tan. He looked a different man from the one who had driven through the bush with her. Back then he had been the tough adventurer, ruggedly handsome. This man was sophisticated, debonair, utterly gorgeous.

She pulled herself up sharply. She shouldn't be thinking like this. Josh Hamilton was a danger zone. Something about him made her senses fall into chaos, made her forget caution and act wildly, irrationally. She couldn't let herself be swept away like that. What she had said to him about her baby was true; she needed to get her life back together and Josh Hamilton spelt heartache.

He looked across and caught her watching him.

'Tea or coffee?'

He smiled. It was a gentle smile that did incredible things to her body temperature. 'Actually, I was hoping you might join me for dinner.' He glanced at his watch. 'I took the liberty of booking a table at Brown's for eight-thirty.'

She should have been annoyed by such presumption. She tried hard to be, and yet there was a small seed of delight that he had asked her.

'Of course, if you're doing something else...' He shrugged. 'It doesn't matter—we'll reschedule.'

He made it sound like some kind of a business meeting. She opened her mouth to refuse the invitation and then to her consternation found herself saying casually, 'I'm not doing anything. Dinner would be lovely.'

The memory of how easy it had been to turn down Harry's invitation earlier nagged in her mind. She'd had absolutely no difficulty in saying no to him, hadn't wanted to accept. Josh Hamilton, however, was a disturbing revelation. She hadn't the strength to refuse him.

She glanced at her watch. 'I'd better go and change.' She gave Josh an uncertain smile. She felt so vulnerable around him. She should be keeping her distance. She should have told him she was washing her hair, she had a date...anything.

'Don't be long,' he said, with an attractive glint in his eye.

In her bedroom, Samantha rifled through her wardrobe with shaking hands. She had very little in the way of expensively stylish clothes. However, she had treated herself to a couple of new suits. Her hand lingered on one that was a shade of hyacinth-blue which matched her eyes. The skirt was a little shorter than she normally wore but it had a long-line jacket that made it into a very smart outfit.

Without examining her reasons for wanting to look her best, she snatched it off the hanger.

It seemed strange sitting next to Josh in the deep luxurious comfort of an Aston Martin in such heavy traffic. She couldn't help casting her mind back to the rough journey they had made together in Africa.

She darted a nervous sideways glance at him. This new, stylish image of his was a bit disconcerting. He looked so different. Incredibly attractive. More attractive than a man had a right to look.

'So, how do you like being back in London?' he asked, turning his head and meeting her gaze.

'It's different.' She smiled shyly. 'I don't know if I'm fully adjusted yet. A car backfired outside the flat the other day and I nearly dived for cover under the coffee-table.'

Josh smiled. 'It will take some time to adjust. Really you could do with a spell in the countryside—right away from everything so that you can just relax.'

She shook her head. 'We're too busy at the agency.'

He paused momentarily. 'I'm surprised that you took that job.'

'Why?'

'Well, it's very different from what you're used to.'

'Yes, it is. But I'm not so sure that I want to go back to nursing. The agency is filling a gap very nicely at the moment.'

'And afterwards, when the baby is born...what do you intend to do then?'

The quietly asked question made her nerves twist. Most of the time she was excited and confident about how she would manage when the baby came along, but there were moments of anxiety. She knew that bringing up a child alone wasn't going to be easy. 'I...I don't know.' Her voice reflected a certain amount of vulnerability for just a second, before she said more brightly, 'But I'm very capable and very resourceful. I'm sure I'll manage. Harry is very keen for me to stay on with the agency.'

'I'm sure he is.' The aridity in Josh's tone did not escape Samantha's notice.

'Believe it or not, I am very good at my job,' she said, very sharply and defensively. 'Harry Unwin would never have offered it to me if he didn't think I was capable.'

'If you say so.'

Samantha didn't like the way he sounded unconvinced. 'Are you trying to suggest that Harry offered me the job because he's attracted to me?' Her voice rose sharply. 'Because if so I find the innuendo insulting and reprehensible. Harry Unwin is a very respectable man who is utterly dedicated to his work. He is caring and—'

'When you've finished canonising Harry, perhaps we could get back down to earth for a moment,' Josh cut across her sardonically. 'The fact is that the job at the agency must be stressful for you. There are constant reminders of Nuangar and Ben. Surely you would be better away from that?'

'I'm coping.' She shrugged. 'And anyway, it isn't so easy to just walk into a good job nowadays.'

'Do you have to work? I'm sure Ben would have wanted you to take things easy.'

'I can't afford to take things easy.' Her tone was abrupt.

'Won't Ben's parents help? Money is certainly no problem for Sarah and Edward, and as you're expecting their grandchild—'

'I like to be independent.' Samantha stared mutinously ahead, her heart pounding unevenly.

'Have you even talked to Sarah about this?' he asked patiently, ignoring her frosty manner completely.

Samantha shrugged. She had seen Ben's parents once since arriving back in London, and she had found the meeting extremely stressful. Sarah Walker had spoken in a brittle non-stop way about Ben and how he would have wanted his child brought up. She had even told Samantha what school to put the baby's name down for and that she should do it right away!

Samantha hadn't had the heart to tell her that Ben hadn't even wanted his child.

Then it had been firmly suggested that Samantha move in with the Walkers and that they get a suitable nanny for the baby. To their outrage Samantha had politely turned down the offer. She had the feeling that if she accepted any help from Sarah and Edward her baby would be taken over.

'I can manage, Josh,' she said firmly. 'And I would be happy if you would just leave the subject there.'

'You are a damned stubborn woman, do you know that?'

She shrugged her shoulders, unperturbed, then firmly changed the subject. 'Tell me, how were things in the north of Nuangar?'

'It was no garden party.' His mouth slanted in a grim smile. 'Put it this way—it made our trip to Salanga look like a fairground ride.'

Samantha grimaced. 'Was your partner all right?'

'Partner?' For a moment he looked puzzled.

'The camerawoman,' Samantha murmured vaguely.

'Oh, Jenny.' He nodded. 'She was fine. Jenny works for the BBC; she knows how to handle herself.'

Had Jenny fallen under Josh's spell like every other woman who seemed to come in contact with him? Samantha was filled with an almost overwhelming urge to ask. She bit the question back and said instead, 'Well, I'm glad you're back safe and sound.'

He pulled the car into a parking space and then turned to look at her. His eyes raked over her smooth complexion and the large, glimmering beauty of her eyes. 'Are you?'

The husky way he spoke those words, the way he was looking at her made the atmosphere between them suddenly charged with electricity. She was reminded vividly of how she had felt at the Salanga hotel, how she had wanted to melt every time he'd touched her, how a deep, undeniable yearning had started just with a glance from those eyes. A little voice started singing inside her head— Danger, danger, danger.

'Of course I am.' She tried desperately to sound light-hearted, but she knew damn fine that her voice was unsteady. She turned away and reached for the doorhandle. All he had said were two little words and they had sounded to her ears like a seduction. Lord, she was going to have to be careful around this man.

'Samantha?' His voice halted her and she looked back at him uncertainly.

Before he could say anything further they were interrupted by the ring of his mobile phone.

'Damn.' Josh grimaced. 'I should have turned that thing off. I foolishly mentioned that I was having a relaxing evening at Brown's when I was talking to my editor on the phone this morning. She probably has other ideas. No rest for the wicked.'

He flashed a smile at her and picked up the phone. His tone was briskly impatient to start with, then it changed abruptly. 'No, you did the right thing,' he said reassuringly.

'Problems?' Samantha asked as he put the phone back down, his expression thoughtful.

'I don't know.' He spoke slowly, his mind elsewhere. 'Apparently my ex-wife is in London. She's just been in to the paper looking for me. She said it was urgent so they told her I would be at Brown's.'

'I hope everything's all right with your son,' Samantha said immediately.

'So do I.' Josh's voice was grim. 'But we'll soon find out. She's on her way down here, apparently.'

Samantha's eyes widened in surprise.

CHAPTER SEVEN

DESPITE the beautiful surroundings, the good food, Samantha didn't actually feel hungry. Irrationally she kept wondering what Josh had been going to say to her before they had been interrupted by that telephone call.

'This meal is a lot different from the one we had in Salanga.' She tried to make light conversation.

'You're not kidding.' Josh smiled across at her, a devilish glint in his eye. 'But dessert was pretty good over there.'

'We didn't have...' Too late she realised he was talking about what had happened between them after dinner. She felt her cheeks flare with colour.

'No, we didn't,' he agreed with a grin. 'But it was still pretty good.'

'You know, Josh, I think we should agree to forget about that.' She hoped she didn't sound as embarrassed as she felt.

'If you say so.' His voice was lazily indifferent.

He was just teasing her; she knew that. She wished now she had just let the remark pass, without sounding so uptight.

She noticed his eyes flicking towards the door a few times. Despite his laid-back attitude he was obviously concerned about Alex, and worried about why his ex-wife had suddenly turned up in London. 'I'm sure everything will be all right with your son,' she said suddenly, in an attempt to reassure him.

He turned his eyes back to her. 'Sophie does tend to veer towards the dramatic. She probably just wants to tell me that she's doing a front cover for *Vogue*.'

Samantha smiled. 'Are you still on good terms with her?'

'Yes.' He nodded. 'Better to be mature about these things. We've both got Alex's best interests at heart.'

'How long since you last saw him?'

'Too long.' He sighed. 'I managed to get over to Paris for Christmas.'

'It's a long separation.'

He nodded grimly. 'He's eight years of age, growing up fast and I'm not there for him.'

Samantha's heart thumped painfully against her chest.

'But I suppose it's my own fault.' He sat back in his chair.

Samantha frowned, not following his logic at all.

'I should have moved to Paris a long time ago, but I made a conscious decision not to.' He reached for his glass. 'When I lost the court case I sat down and thought about it and I came to the conclusion that I had my own life to live. I couldn't spend it following Sophie around from place to place as the mood took her, no matter how much I loved my child.' His lips twisted drily. 'It was a miscalculation.'

Samantha shook her head. 'I don't follow you...'

'Well, I figured that my ex-wife's infatuation with Bernard wouldn't last and that she would be moving on very soon.'

'As soon as he had relaunched her modelling career?' Samantha hazarded the guess as she remembered his saying something to that effect in Nuangar.

He nodded. 'Sophie was always a bit flighty—very impulsive and very unpredictable...or rather she used to be. Obviously she has settled down.'

'Are they qualities that you admire in a woman?' Samantha asked without thinking.

He frowned.

'I'm not being funny,' she said hastily. 'It's just that you said she was always flighty...always impulsive. Yet you married her.'

'You're quite right.' For a moment he grinned. 'I did know those things about her before we married. At the time I found them exciting. She was—in fact still is— incredibly sexy.'

Samantha felt the painful thrust of some alien emotion inside her. It was like a knife twisting.

'In my defence, I was young and I was turned on by her fabulous body and glamorous good looks.' Josh shrugged. 'I'm ashamed to say I didn't look very much deeper.'

'Not very commendable,' Samantha muttered sharply.

One dark eyebrow lifted. 'I made a terrible mistake... but it's not exactly uncommon.'

'Oh, I'm sorry, Josh!' Samantha bit sharply down on her lip. Why had she reacted so angrily to his words? When he had said that he still found Sophie incredibly sexy she had actually seen a red-hot blaze of light across her eyelids.

'Well, I suppose you're right in a way...I should have known better.' He grimaced. 'It's just grossly unfair that Alex has to pay for my mistakes.'

'You can't blame yourself for everything,' Samantha said gently. 'No matter how hard anyone tries, life isn't all neat edges. And anyway, Alex isn't unhappy—you said so yourself.'

'No, he's not.' Josh shook his head, then frowned. 'I wonder if he's here in London.'

The waiter arrived and removed their plates, then placed their main courses in front of them.

'Pretty grim admitting to you that lust was one of the primary incentives that sent me rushing to the altar like a lemming,' Josh said once they were left alone again.

'Pretty grim,' she agreed with a small smile.

'You never talk about Ben,' Josh said suddenly. 'Is it because it upsets you too much to talk about him, or is it just that you don't want to discuss him with me?'

Her heart thumped violently at the direct question. 'What do you want me to say?' She was instantly on the defensive; she could hear it herself.

His eyes moved over the paleness of her skin, the wide blue eyes.

'Say what's in your heart,' he urged softly. 'I think that would be a good place to start.'

She swallowed hard. Her marriage had been a mistake too. With every day that went by she could see that more clearly. But admitting such a thing out loud was hard.

'Where did you meet him?' Josh prompted as the silence grew.

'When I went to work in Chuanga.' Her lips felt stiff; they didn't want to form the words.

'And it was love at first sight?' Josh prompted again when she didn't continue.

For a moment she just looked at him. She wanted to be able to say yes; she really did.

'Samantha?' he said, and she shook her head.

'We just sort of seemed to drift together. Things were very bad in Chuanga in that period. The town was under constant siege every day.'

Her voice wavered precariously as she remembered the full horror for a moment. 'Ben helped me keep my sanity.'

'Sounds grim.'

She nodded. 'Marrying Ben Walker was like grabbing hold of a life-jacket in the middle of the ocean in a force-ten gale.'

'And when the storm subsided you realised that you had made the right decision, even though it was made during a time of stress?'

That question made her swallow hard. It was too perceptive...too deep. 'Of course.' Her voice cracked hollowly.

'You must miss him a lot.'

'Josh?' A husky voice interrupted them and Samantha looked up.

A beautiful young woman in her late twenties stood next to the table. She had dark, Latin-type looks—long hair lay in luxurious waves around her face, her eyes were dark and smouldering and her lips, by contrast, were vivid scarlet. She wore a red suit with a short skirt and a fitted jacket. The outfit showed off incredibly long legs and a superb figure which was both voluptuous and slender.

'Hello, Sophie.' Josh's voice was level and courteous.

This was Josh's ex-wife! Samantha shouldn't have been taken aback. Josh had told her that Sophie was attractive...sexy. It was just that she hadn't been prepared for her to look quite so glamorous. She had a polished sheen of sophistication and wealth, as if she spent all her time in beauty salons and fashion houses.

'Did the paper manage to get in contact with you?' the woman asked nervously. 'They told me that I would find you here.'

Josh nodded. 'How's Alex? Is he with you?'

'He's fine. My mother's looking after him.'

One eyebrow lifted. 'So he's here in London?'

'Yes. We arrived this afternoon.' Sophie slanted a curious glance at Samantha. In a moment her eyes weighed up her clothes and her hair, then she turned her attention firmly back to her ex-husband. 'Look, do you think I could talk privately to you, Josh?' she asked in a low, drawling tone.

Josh looked across at Samantha, a wry expression on his face.

'I'd like you to meet my ex-wife,' he said smoothly. 'Samantha, this is Sophie.'

The woman looked at her again and just nodded. Then she continued swiftly with her conversation, as if the introduction hadn't taken place. 'It's really important, Josh.'

'Is it about Alex?'

The woman hesitated, and it was immediately apparent that it was something along much more personal lines that was bothering her. 'Well, indirectly,' she said.

Samantha, who was feeling most uncomfortable by now, felt obliged to interrupt. 'Perhaps I should get a taxi home and—'

'Certainly not.' Josh's voice left no room for argument. He glanced up at his ex-wife. 'What is all this about, Sophie?'

'Can I sit down?' Sophie didn't wait for his agreement but looked about her for a spare chair. Immediately a waiter came over to help her and then took her order for a large gin and tonic.

'I've left Bernard.'

The words fell into the silence as soon as the waiter had left them.

Josh leaned back in his chair and surveyed the woman through narrowed lashes. 'Why?'

'We haven't been getting along.' Sophie pushed an impatient hand through her hair. 'It's a long story. But I'm back to live in London for good.'

It was hard to tell what Josh made of this piece of news; his face was an interesting study in inscrutability. 'How's Alex taking it?'

'He's fine. In fact he's very excited about being back here.' Sophie put a slender hand on Josh's in an impulsive and intimate way. 'But we've got to talk, Josh. I know you've always tried to keep in close contact with us over the years…and I haven't made things easy.'

'You know, Sophie, now isn't a real good time for us to go through this.' Josh's voice was firm.

'I suppose…' Her voice lowered to a husky, attractive level. 'It's just that I realise now that I've wasted so much time, and I want to start putting it right as soon as possible. I made a very big mistake in going to Paris with Bernard. Alex needs his father.'

Samantha moved uncomfortably in her chair. She didn't want to be witness to this, and watching the easy way the other woman's hand was resting on Josh's and the way he made no effort to move it was doing strange things to her emotions.

The waiter arrived with Sophie's drink and asked if they would like dessert or coffee as he cleared away the empty plates. Samantha shook her head. She wanted to get out of here; she had no desire to play gooseberry.

'I should really be going,' she said quickly as Josh looked across at her.

'Don't run away on my account,' Sophie put in, and batted wide eyes at Samantha. 'Josh and I have all the time in the world to sort ourselves out.'

Run away? The patronising tone and the way the woman had turned the tables to make *her* feel like the intruder made Samantha bristle. 'Well, in that case I'd love a coffee,' she found herself saying sweetly. She was damned if she was going to excuse herself meekly after that statement.

She was aware that Sophie's expression registered displeasure, however it was hastily masked behind a smile as Josh's attention returned to her.

'So how are you, darling?' she asked nonchalantly. Her hand was now resting lightly on Josh's arm.

Samantha had to admire the woman's gall. It didn't

seem to occur to her that her presence might be unwelcome. But perhaps it wasn't? Samantha watched Josh as he chatted easily with his ex-wife and a curl of envy stirred forcefully to life. It was an emotion she wasn't familiar with and it shocked her totally that she should feel it now. It was just that they looked good together, and Josh was watching Sophie so intently, listening to her with complete concentration.

'We got your last letter,' Sophie was saying now. 'It had a London postmark on it, which threw me a little as you had obviously written it in Africa.'

'Samantha posted it for me.'

'How kind.' Sophie glanced across at her and her eyes narrowed. 'When I received it, I just knew I had to come home.'

Samantha frowned. She knew that letter had been addressed to Alex, yet Sophie made it sound as if it had been for her.

'I take it you are a fellow journalist?' the woman asked now.

'No. I was working for an international aid agency in Nuangar.'

The waiter brought their coffee and then departed discreetly again.

'So you're just back in London on holiday?'

'No, I'm back to stay.' Samantha wasn't about to go into details.

'I don't blame you. It must be tough out there.' Sophie looked back at Josh. 'I know I was worried sick when Josh first started going out to those hostile places.'

Josh shook his head. 'Come on, Sophie,' he said impatiently. 'You were living in Paris with Bernard. I'm sure you didn't give it a second thought.'

'But I did.' Her eyes locked with his. 'I kept wondering

if I had driven you to taking such a dangerous job. I worried about you constantly.'

Josh's lips twisted in an arrogantly amused smile. 'Well, thanks for the concern,' he said laconically, then he pushed his chair back from the table. 'If you ladies will excuse me, I'll just go and see to the bill.' He paused and looked down at Sophie. 'Did you drive over here or get a taxi?'

'I got a taxi, darling. You can drop me off.'

Josh didn't say anything to that.

There was a moment's silence after he had left. Samantha noticed how Sophie's eyes followed Josh across the room; there was a look of contemplation on her face.

'He doesn't believe me, but I never stopped thinking about him,' she murmured when at last she looked back at Samantha. 'And I honestly do believe he took that foreign correspondent job because he was so damn cut up about my leaving him that he didn't care about anything any more.'

'He cared about Alex,' Samantha said quietly.

'Well, that goes without saying. Josh is a wonderful father.' Sophie met her eyes directly. 'Are you dating my husband?'

The question took Samantha aback. She could hardly believe the audacity. 'He's your ex-husband, isn't he?' she managed to ask coolly.

'For now.' Sophie's tone was crystal-clear. 'But I think it's only fair to warn you that I intend to get him back.'

'That's this week's game-plan, is it?' Samantha drawled the words sardonically but she was shocked, and more perturbed by the blunt statement than she had a right to be.

'It might take me a little longer than a week, but not much.' Sophie deliberately misunderstood the dig at her flighty character.

Samantha decided she didn't like anything about Sophie Hamilton. She didn't like her effrontery in just marching in here on a whim. She didn't like the arrogant way she assumed she could easily get Josh back. But most of all she didn't like the way the woman was able to stir up a wave of red-hot jealousy inside her. Some angry spark inside made her say rashly, 'Perhaps I should warn *you* that it might not be as easy to get him back as you seem to think.'

Afterwards she would try to analyse why she had said that. Had it just been a desire to wipe that confident, smug look off Sophie's face or had it been something deeper? Had she been rising to the challenge because she was so attracted to Josh?

Sophie was unperturbed. 'Josh loves me… I've always known I could have him back whenever I wanted.'

Aware that Josh was on his way back across the room, Samantha let the matter drop.

'Well, if you're ready, Samantha, we'll leave,' he said as he reached the table.

Sophie finished her drink and the three of them walked out of the hotel together.

'I rang a taxi for you at Reception,' Josh informed his ex-wife as she hesitated on the front step.

She looked up at him with a kind of helpless, wide-eyed look. 'I told Alex you would come home with me this evening—tuck him up in bed.' She was standing very close to him and her voice was low and intimate, but Samantha could hear every word clearly.

'You shouldn't have told him that, Sophie. It's not fair to the boy to make rash promises.' Josh glanced at his wristwatch, his manner annoyed. 'Besides, he'll be asleep by now.'

'Not when he thinks you'll be coming home.'

The words were heavy with the evocative promise of a family reunited.

Samantha felt a dart of pure anger. Sophie obviously wasn't above using Alex to get her ex-husband back. She glanced at Josh, wondering what he made of the situation. Was he angry...flattered...interested? His face was infuriatingly hard to read.

'Here's your taxi.' He strolled out to open the door of the black cab as it came to a halt beside them.

Samantha couldn't help it; she felt a brief moment of victorious pleasure as she watched Sophie getting into that taxi. At least the woman wasn't going to get everything her own way.

'I take it you're staying with your mother?' Josh asked her as she looked up at him with a hurt expression in her eyes.

'Yes...' Sophie's voice trailed off, and then she said, 'You could call round later—it doesn't matter what time.'

'I'll phone you.' Josh's voice was gentle but it held an undercurrent of taut resolution. 'Give my love to Alex.'

The taxi pulled into the traffic and Josh turned towards Samantha. 'I'm sorry about that.'

'It's OK.' Samantha injected a note of light airiness into her tone but it was an effort.

Josh was very quiet on the way home. Samantha kept glancing surreptitiously at his profile, wondering what he was thinking. Was he wishing he had put her in that taxi instead of Sophie?

'Your wife is very beautiful,' she murmured hesitantly. There was a part of her that didn't know if she wanted to probe that area. Maybe she wouldn't like what he had to say.

'Ex-wife,' Josh corrected her, his eyes on the driving mirror as he negotiated the busy traffic.

He flicked Samantha a sardonic glance as soon as they

stopped at some traffic lights. 'And I thought that she had settled down with Bernard! I could hardly believe it—the words were no sooner out of my mouth than she had waltzed in with those beautiful eyes welling with tears. After all these years, she's still as unpredictable as ever.'

And did he still find that exciting? Samantha's heart seemed to be dancing a strange and rapid painful tattoo. 'Did you ask her to come back in your letter?' She was proud of how casual she had made that question sound.

He frowned at that. 'No, I did not. That letter was strictly for Alex.'

It was amazing how much better that made her feel. 'Well, at least you'll have him nearer to you now,' she said cheerfully.

He nodded. 'Poor kid. I hope all this hasn't upset him too much.'

Silence fell again. Then suddenly he said, 'Do you think she was serious when she said Alex would still be awake, waiting for me?'

'Maybe.' Samantha bit down on her lip. Sophie's ace card had not been played in vain. Alex was certainly the string to pull to get Josh's attention. It was despicable that the woman would stoop so low as to use her son like that. She darted another glance at Josh and then found herself saying bluntly, 'On the other hand she could just have been saying that to get you round to her house.'

'You could be right.' He glanced across at her, a sardonic expression on the handsome features. 'Sophie has mood swings like the British weather.'

He pulled up outside her flat and got out of the car to walk with her to the front door.

The weather had cleared now, and it was a fine warm evening. A breeze snatched at the cherry trees that lined the street and blew pink blossom across the pavement like confetti.

'You got your wish,' Josh said gently as they stopped outside her front door.

'What's that?'

'You're back home for the cherry blossom.'

She smiled at that, remembering how she had spoken wistfully in Salanga about England. 'You've got a good memory for trivia.'

'Only important trivia.' He reached out and touched her face, his fingers gentle against the curve of her cheek. She moistened her lips nervously, her heart thumping rapidly against her chest. For a moment she thought he was going to kiss her, and the depth of her longing to feel his lips against hers was sudden and intense.

'Would you like to come inside?' Her voice was uncertain, as was the way she looked up at him. The feelings he so unexpectedly created inside her made her feel so vulnerable...so frightened.

'I don't think I'd better.' He dropped his hand from her skin. 'I've got an hour's drive back out to my house.'

Disappointment was acute and she hated herself for it. 'That's if you manage to get there.' She spoke without thinking.

One dark eyebrow lifted at that and she shrugged airily. 'Well, I suppose you'll be driving home via Sophie's house?'

'Ah-h-h!' There was a glint of devilment in his eyes at that, and his lips curved in an enigmatic smile. 'Anyone would think you were jealous, Samantha.'

'Don't be absurd!' White-hot heat swept through her at that mocking tone...at the fact that he was so right. 'I'm not the slightest bit bothered who you—'

Before she could say anything else he bent his head and kissed her full on the lips.

The action made her senses swim. His lips were warm, sensual, inviting—and she responded instinctively. It felt so good to be close to him. She ached for his arms to go around her, for him to hold her close and deepen the kiss even further. She felt desolate when he moved away.

'Goodnight, Samantha.'

She watched as he walked away from her and memories of Africa stirred deep inside. Of how he had kissed and caressed her naked body, of how deeply she had wanted him. Of how she had felt when he'd walked away from her at the Salanga airfield. Those feelings hadn't been in her imagination; they were no mere fantasy.

He got into his car and she turned away, consumed with the aching knowledge that he was going to Sophie.

CHAPTER EIGHT

'THAT computer course is in two weeks.' Harry's voice
was cool.

Samantha frowned. She had noticed that Harry's manner had been unusually abrupt and withdrawn this morning, but until now she hadn't had time to think about it
because things in the office had been so busy.

'That's the address and the itinerary.' He put a sheet of
paper in front of her on her desk and she skimmed through
it quickly.

He lowered his tone. 'I tried to ring you last night.'

She was barely listening to him; her eyes were too busy
taking in the fact that the course was in the Midlands.
'Yes, I was out... Harry, this course is miles away! You
didn't say that I would have to travel so far.'

'It's no problem. I'm arranging transport and accom-
modation.' His voice was dismissive. 'So where were you
last night? I thought you were staying in, having an early
night?'

Samantha looked up sharply. There was a note in
Harry's voice that sounded suspiciously like annoyance.
She hoped sincerely that she was mistaken...that Josh's
remarks last night had been wrong. 'I changed my mind
and went out.' Her voice was cool with displeasure.
'That's all right, isn't it? I don't have to clear it with the
office first?'

'No...no, don't be silly,' he blustered, obviously taken
aback by her frosty manner. 'It was just that I'd forgotten

to give you a message. Josh Hamilton rang you yesterday morning and it slipped my mind completely until I got home.'

'Oh, I'm sorry, Harry.' Samantha immediately felt awful for jumping to the wrong conclusions and snapping at him. It was all Josh's fault, she thought with annoyance. He had planted those seeds of insanity about Harry being infatuated by her. 'I think I must be overtired. It's all right about Josh—he caught up with me at my flat last night.'

'That's OK, then.' Harry turned away and went back through to his office.

Samantha watched him go with a feeling of guilt. She shouldn't have been so abrupt. She hadn't been lying when she had told him she was overtired. She had hardly slept last night—her mind had been going over and over the situation between Josh and his ex-wife. Had he gone to Sophie after dropping her off?

Samantha returned her attention to her computer screen. She wasn't going to give Josh Hamilton another thought, she told herself fiercely. She had a lot of work to get through before lunch. There was no time to waste on Josh.

Even so, annoying thoughts of Sophie and him kept popping into her head. Pictures of them entwined in each other's arms. The memory of Sophie telling her that getting him back was going to be quick and easy.

She made a few errors on the computer and cursed herself for allowing herself to be distracted. After that she made a determined effort to shut everything out except her work, but it took all her will-power, all her strength.

When she heard the outer door of the office opening she glanced up. Her eyes widened and her attention was hooked when she saw Josh Hamilton strolling in.

He was wearing a dark suit which emphasised the powerful lines of his body, and he looked so attractive that

Samantha could feel her heart dip up and down as if someone had just hit it with a baseball bat.

'Samantha, how are you this morning?' His voice was deep and polite, and the other girls in the office glanced over. Samantha could see them out of the corner of her eye as they did a kind of double take at just how handsome he was.

'I'm fine; how are you?' She was proud of how cool and businesslike she sounded.

'Better for seeing you.' He grinned and her heart dipped crazily again. She hated herself for allowing him to affect her like this. She couldn't understand the dangerous kind of passion he seemed to arouse in her with just a look, a few words.

'So what can I do for you?' She managed to maintain the air of indifference with extreme difficulty.

'Actually, I'm here in my professional capacity to see your boss.'

Samantha refused to acknowledge the brutal kick of disappointment that seemed to lodge itself deep inside. She couldn't care less, she told herself angrily. She hadn't expected him to want to see her and she didn't give a damn. 'Have you got an appointment?'

'No...but I was hoping I could sweet-talk you into letting me see him anyway.'

She wondered why he wanted to speak to Harry, but she wouldn't ask. 'Sounds like bribery of the lowest kind,' she murmured flippantly. 'Usually I expect flawless diamonds... However, just for you...' She reached for her phone to buzz into Harry's office.

He sounded less than pleased about the interruption, but he agreed after a moment's hesitation.

'He'll be a few minutes,' Samantha told Josh as she replaced the receiver.

'Thanks.' Much to her consternation he perched himself on the edge of her desk.

She turned her attention back to her work and tried to forget he was there.

'You seem busy,' he remarked laconically.

'I've got a few things I want to finish before lunch.' She didn't glance up at him.

'How about if we have lunch together?' he asked casually. 'I was planning on going for something to eat after seeing Harry.'

For a moment she was tempted…sorely tempted. Then she remembered Sophie. She couldn't allow herself to get dragged into that triangle…couldn't risk falling for someone who was in love with someone else. She had been there and done that. With Ben she hadn't realised the situation…with Josh she could see it clearly. She would be a fool not to have learnt by her mistake.

'I'm sorry, I've already made plans for lunch.' It took all her strength to refuse him and she couldn't bring herself to look him in the eye.

'This reminds me of the first time we met…do you remember? You were so busy, you had no time to see me.'

'I had a lot of patients to attend to.' Her voice was curt, but she did remember. She recalled vividly how attractive she had found him from the first moment their eyes had met. What had it been…chemistry? Whatever it had been, it had scared her then…had annoyed her intensely. It frightened the hell out of her now.

'I thought you were the perfect nurse…very sexy.' He drawled the words, making no attempt to lower his voice.

Samantha glared up at him, her skin flooding with hot colour. 'And I thought you were the perfect nuisance.'

He smiled, unperturbed. 'And now here you are the perfect, very attractive secretary.'

'I'm not a secretary.' She glared up at him.

He shrugged. 'But you are very attractive.' His tone was warm and velvety. She knew he was deliberately winding her up, that he was well aware that all the other women in the office were listening.

'You're infuriating.' She dropped her voice to a very low level. 'Tell me, how is your wife this morning?' The pointed question just appeared, without her even thinking about it.

'Alas, I have no wife.' He spread his hands, a rueful, teasing glint in his eye. 'But if you mean Sophie, then as far as I'm aware she's as beautiful and outrageous as she was yesterday at dinner.'

She felt a vicious thrust of emotion at those words. Did he have to keep saying how beautiful Sophie was? 'You mean you didn't see her after you dropped me off?' She hadn't wanted to ask that question, but she'd had to; it had been burning a hole inside her.

He looked amused now. 'Is that why you refused my invitation to lunch? Because you think I went round and spent the night with my ex-wife last night?'

'You're very conceited.' Her voice was a low hiss of fury. She hated him in that moment—hated him because he was right, because she was eaten up with jealousy. 'Actually, I couldn't care less what you do. I've got a lunch-date.' She lied through her teeth in an angry attempt to salvage her pride, then promptly wished she hadn't. Now he probably wouldn't bother to ask her out again. But that was what she wanted...wasn't it?

For an unguarded moment uncertainty and vulnerability showed clearly in her wide blue eyes as she looked up at him.

'Who with?'

She didn't answer him. She couldn't bring herself to

dig herself deeper in and make up a name. She was very relieved when Harry interrupted them.

'Sorry to keep you waiting, Josh.'

'That's OK. Samantha has been keeping me entertained.'

Samantha cringed. Had her lie been totally transparent?

The two men went through to the other office and closed the door. Immediately one of the other girls across the room called out, 'Who is he, Samantha?'

'Josh Hamilton. He's a journalist.' She tried to focus her attention on the screen in front of her.

'He's gorgeous!'

Samantha pretended she hadn't heard that. Another woman falling to Josh's charms, she thought with bitter irony. He had probably broken more hearts than there were days in a year. She was well out of it, she told herself firmly. Even so her hands trembled slightly as she started back to work on her keyboard, and there was an ache deep down that wouldn't go away.

As time passed and Josh was still in Harry's office she kept flicking glances over towards the door, her curiosity becoming more and more aroused. What were they talking about?

They both emerged a while later. 'Thanks, Josh, I'll look into that,' Harry was saying.

Samantha glanced up at the two men, and then frowned. Was it her imagination or did Harry look somewhat flustered? She watched as the two men shook hands and then her boss returned into his office, leaving Josh to find his way out.

She pretended not to be interested as he walked towards her desk.

'My home number and my work number.' Josh put two cards down in front of her. 'If you want anything, or need to talk about anything, give me a call.'

Samantha looked up in surprise. 'What would I need to talk about?'

His lips twisted in a grin. 'Anything you want...the price of fish, if it turns you on.'

'Thanks, I'll bear it in mind,' she said drily, her fingers playing nervously with the cards. Was this his way of saying goodbye...of telling her he wouldn't be getting in contact again?

'As I can't interest you in lunch, how about dinner one day next week?'

The casually offered invitation made her heart soar upwards.

'Well...I...' She wanted to accept. She wanted to say that it would be lovely. But she was afraid of the consequences of seeing him. She was so strongly attracted, like a child fascinated by fire.

They were interrupted by a woman's voice. 'Hello, Samantha. I haven't caught you at a bad time, have I?'

'Aunt Sylvia!' Samantha looked over at her aunt, startled to see her. 'I didn't even hear the office door opening.'

'Well, you did seem somewhat preoccupied.' Sylvia was an attractive woman in her early fifties. Her blonde hair was skilfully styled and she had a trim figure. She cast an interested glance at Josh and immediately he extended a hand and introduced himself.

'I'm relieved that you're Samantha's lunch-date,' he said with a twinkle in his eye. 'I was starting to think she was seeing another man.'

She could see Sylvia opening her mouth to say that she had only called on the spur of the moment, then closing it again in case she was putting her foot in things.

'So how about dinner next week, Samantha?' Josh invited.

Samantha noticed he wasn't inviting her out this weekend. Was the prime time of Saturday night reserved for Sophie? 'How about a week on Saturday?' she found herself saying casually, just to see if he would agree.

He hesitated for just a moment before nodding his head. 'That would be fine. I'll pick you up at seven-thirty.' Then he smiled at Sylvia. 'It was nice meeting you,' he said politely.

'And you.' Sylvia watched as he went out of the office, and then as soon as the door closed behind him she turned to her niece with an expressive look of approval on her face. 'Wow!' was all she said.

'Yes, he is attractive, isn't he?' Samantha tried to keep her voice carefully neutral as she switched off her computer and reached for her bag.

'Attractive? He's a positive hunk.'

Samantha suppressed a smile. 'Have you called to do lunch?'

Sylvia nodded. 'If you've got time?' She frowned. 'What was all that about another man?'

'Nothing.' Samantha waved that away airily. 'Come on, I'm dying to get out of here.'

It was a relief to get out in the fresh air. They walked to a little Italian restaurant on the corner, and the whole way Sylvia kept up her conversation about Josh.

Samantha managed to change the subject a couple of times, but as they took their seats in a corner booth of the restaurant her aunt firmly turned it back.

Was Josh single? How long did she think he was back in London for?

'I've no idea.' Samantha picked up the menu. 'To be honest, Sylvia, his ex-wife is back on the scene and I think they might get back together.' She tried to sound indifferent.

'So why on earth did you make a date for over a week

away?' Sylvia asked with exasperation. 'A faint heart never won a fabulous man.'

'I thought that was a fair maiden?' Samantha corrected her wryly.

'Do you care if you lose him to his ex-wife?'

The quietly asked question made her look up and meet her aunt's eyes. She wished she could say no, but the truth of the matter was that she did care. The very thought of his getting back with Sophie made her heart squeeze painfully.

Sylvia reached out and took her hand as she saw the answer very clearly in her niece's eyes. 'You don't get many chances at happiness in this life, Sam. When one presents itself you should grab it with both hands. Otherwise you might just regret it for the rest of your life.'

Samantha's eyes clouded. 'I'm just so scared, Sylvia,' she admitted huskily. 'I made a mistake once before. I don't want to be hurt again... And there is my baby to consider. My child has to come first...before my own needs,' she said with passionate emphasis.

Sylvia nodded. 'But denying yourself happiness isn't going to help your child, is it? You deserve to be happy.' Sylvia squeezed her hand. 'Don't wait over a week to see him, Samantha.'

For two days Samantha held off ringing Josh, but he was never out of her mind. It was early on Sunday evening when she finally summoned up the courage to pick up the phone. As she listened to it ringing she went over and over what she should say—Just wondered if we could fit dinner in a little earlier this week? She'd sound really casual, as if it was no big deal.

The phone was picked up and her heartbeats increased at the warm prospect of hearing Josh's voice. But it was a woman who answered. There was a moment when she hoped she had the wrong number, then there was a horrible feeling of bitter disappointment as she recognised Sophie Hamilton's voice.

For a second she contemplated throwing down the receiver, but she forced herself to ask to speak to Josh.

'Who shall I say is calling?' Sophie asked coolly.

'Samantha Walker.'

Sophie put down the phone and she could hear her calling, 'Darling, it's that work colleague for you.'

Samantha had never experienced such jealousy—it curled through her in waves. What was Sophie doing round at Josh's house…were they reconciled?

'Samantha, hello.' Josh sounded genuinely pleased to hear from her as he lifted the phone.

Obviously it was a front, she thought angrily. 'Have I caught you at a bad time?' She tried desperately to take the cutting edge out of her tone, but she could hear it there all the same.

'No. Sophie and Alex are here and we're just going through some brochures on schools in the London area.'

It sounded very cosy. There was an awkward silence as she wondered what she should say next.

'You're not ringing up to cancel our date on Saturday, are you?'

Hope flared amidst her confusion. If he could speak so openly about them having a 'date', perhaps he had no intention of getting back with his ex-wife? 'Well, no…I was just wondering if we could change the day?'

'How about tomorrow night?'

The heat of Africa seemed to lick through her veins and she smiled. 'That would be fine.'

'Darling, your supper is getting cold.' Sophie's husky tones penetrated very clearly down the line to Samantha.

'So I'll pick you up at seven-thirty,' Josh told her, completely ignoring his ex-wife.

'Seven-thirty,' Samantha agreed. Her heart thumped painfully as she put the receiver down. Just what in the hell was going on around there? she wondered in anguish as she stared at the phone.

CHAPTER NINE

JOSH picked her up exactly on time. He was dressed smartly but casually in a pair of fawn trousers and an open-necked patterned shirt.

She was pleased that she had resisted the impulse to overdress for the occasion and had opted for a simple blue Laura Ashley dress.

'You look lovely,' Josh said as they made their way out to his car.

'Thank you.' She knew she was looking well. Pregnancy had given her a healthy glow and she was carrying the baby very neatly. She was in her fourteenth week now and it barely showed. Her dress fitted into her tiny waist and then flowed in feminine loose billows around her legs.

'I thought we would eat at my place, if that's all right with you?' he said as he opened the passenger door for her. 'It's just that I'm expecting an important telephone call and I'd rather take it at home than in a restaurant.'

'It's fine by me,' she said easily.

He flashed her a smile. 'I'm a good cook, so you're perfectly safe.'

'I never doubted it for a moment.' A tremor of apprehension belied her light-hearted tone. Suddenly she was remembering what had happened after dinner in Salanga.

She was silent for a while as Josh drove through the heavy traffic. Earlier she had promised herself that she wouldn't mention his ex-wife too much. That she wouldn't ask all the questions that had kept her awake at night. She didn't want him to know just how eaten away by suspicion and jealousy she was.

'So how is Alex?' she asked brightly as they left the city behind.

'He's in good spirits. Excited about being back in England.'

'You must be relieved to have him back so close.'

'I am, believe me.' He turned the car down a narrow country lane, then between high gateposts.

A large detached residence of considerable style and character sat regally in the midst of a beautifully set out garden. Evergreen ivy spread its tenacious fingers over rustic brick, and mullioned windows glinted in the early-evening sunshine.

The size of the place surprised Samantha. This was no bachelor pad; it was a family home.

The inside was as impressive as the outside. Open rustic brickwork and oak beams gave it the feel of the country. Vases of fresh flowers reflected in highly polished tables and a chintz suite sat elegantly on beige carpets. Everything was very orderly and a lot of attention had been paid to detail.

'Are you sure you live here alone?' Samantha remarked as he led her through the hall and into a large kitchen in rich pine. The place was spotless, the counters and split-level cooker gleaming as if they had been polished for hours. 'By the looks of things you've got an army of women installed to keep the place like this.'

He laughed at that. 'That's a sexist remark if ever I heard one. But I have got one woman to help me.' He started to get out pots and pans from cupboards. 'Mrs Brown. She doesn't live in, except during the summer holidays, when Alex comes to stay and I need extra help.'

'Maybe you won't need her as much this year,'

Samantha said as she sat down on one of the high kitchen stools and watched him working.

'Why's that?'

'Well…with Sophie being back in England.' She ventured on bravely. 'I suppose she'll be spending a lot of time here again…she was here last night.' She could have bitten out her tongue as soon as she'd said the words—after all her resolutions not to say too much!

Josh glanced across at her and she met his eyes with a wide blue innocent look. All right, so she wanted to know what was happening between him and his ex-wife, she told herself crossly, but it was nothing more than natural female curiosity.

'Mrs Brown worked for me when I was married to Sophie. I've had her for years, and unless she decides to retire I'd say I'll have her whatever happens.'

It wasn't much of an answer. What did he mean by 'whatever happens'? Samantha wondered.

'So, did you sort out a school for Alex last night?' She couldn't leave the subject, even though she knew she was in danger of sounding too interested.

'I think so.' Josh opened the fridge and took some salad ingredients out. 'We made an appointment and went to see Rothschild's this morning. Alex seemed to like it a lot.'

'And is Sophie happy with the way things are going?' she asked quietly.

'She seems a bit confused at the moment.'

Was she going for the sympathy vote? Samantha wondered drily. It certainly seemed to be working. Josh had sounded sorry for her.

Samantha looked down at her hands. She had no reason to care how much time Josh spent with his ex-wife, yet she did. That appalling feeling of jealousy was so strong that it was almost overwhelming.

'Well, I hope things work out for her.' She forced the words out politely.

'I'm sure they will. Apparently Bernard didn't like the constant restraints that having a child around involved...that was a contributing part of their relationship break-up. We've had a long talk and she seems determined to make things work in England now, for Alex's sake. Sophie's changed quite a bit.'

The confidence in his tone totally threw her. Was Josh prepared to have his ex-wife back for Alex's sake? It sounded as if it was a definite possibility. He loved his child, and if he still had feelings for Sophie it would probably work out.

Why did it hurt so much? She couldn't comprehend the feelings that his words had stirred up inside her at all. Since her conversation with Sylvia she had admitted to herself that if Josh got back with his ex-wife it would upset her. But she had been totally unprepared for this feeling of utter devastation.

'Sam?' Josh's gentle voice brought her out of her reverie, and she realised that he had just said something else to her and she hadn't heard a word of it.

She forced a bright smile to her face. 'Sorry, I was miles away. I was just thinking how lucky Alex is,' she said lightly, 'to have a father who cares so deeply about him.'

She would never have admitted it, but she had also been thinking how lucky Sophie was. For a moment there was a feeling of such bleakness inside her that she knew it must show in her eyes. She stood up before he could make any reply. 'How about my giving you a hand with dinner?' She forced herself to sound cheerful. 'I can't just sit here while you do all the work.'

'Of course you can. You're the honoured guest.' Smoothly Josh reached for the bottle that was chilling in an ice bucket beside him. 'Take a drink and relax in the other room for a while.'

She hoped fervently that he wasn't aware of how much their conversation had just upset her. It would be too shameful by far. 'Only if it's non-alcoholic.' She smiled.

'I wouldn't offer you anything else.' He poured her a glass. 'I asked Mrs Brown to lay the table in the conservatory. Go through and make yourself comfortable.'

It was a relief to turn away from him. She desperately needed a moment alone to compose herself.

The door he had indicated led through to an enormous Edwardian-style conservatory. The sun was starting to go down now, and the last dying rays of pink reflected off the silver cutlery and crystal on a table set in the midst of a riot of tropical flowers and plants.

Samantha didn't sit down on one of the comfortable wicker chairs; instead she stood at the windows, looking out over the back garden.

The place was a picture of beauty. A well-manicured lawn swept down towards the River Thames and weeping willows trailed their fronds into the cool blue water. Beside some colourful flowerbeds there was a swing and a slide and a paved area with a basketball net. Samantha closed her eyes against a sudden image of Josh and Sophie playing out there with their son.

She rested the side of her face against the chill of her glass in an attempt to cool her heated countenance. Then she tried to analyse the wayward emotions inside her calmly.

She was in love with Josh Hamilton. The stark truth was undeniable. The way she had felt when he had talked about his ex-wife just now could leave her under no illusions about that.

When had it happened? she wondered dazedly. The first

KATHRYN ROSS   125

time she had seen him on that hospital ward? When they'd been alone together in the bush? When?

She remembered how she had told herself that her feelings for him weren't real...that she was lonely, that she was on the rebound. She almost laughed bitterly aloud. Rebound from what? She had never known this total feeling of love for Ben, had never experienced such total, overwhelming passion that she wanted to melt every time he touched her. This wasn't anything to do with loneliness.

She loved everything about Josh. She loved the way he raised his eyebrows and fixed her with that laughing look of his. She loved the deep tenderness in his voice when he spoke about his son. The depth of her need for him was immense. If someone had offered her one wish at this moment she would have asked that he return those feelings.

'It's getting dark.' Josh's velvet tones from behind her made her turn hurriedly.

He put their meal on the table and then lit the candles. The air of intimacy the flickering light gave out was enough to make her want to turn and run to switch on the overhead lights. Her sensitive emotions didn't need candlelight.

He pulled out a chair for her and looked at her questioningly.

From somewhere she found the strength to try and behave normally. She sat gracefully in the chair and complimented him on the meal, which did look wonderful.

'Why did you come in to see Harry on Friday?' she asked as he took the chair opposite. It was the only topic of conversation that she could think of that wasn't emotionally loaded.

He shrugged. 'Just a piece of information I wanted to check for a news item.'

For a second she thought she heard an undertone in his voice. It was very strange, but she had sensed a similar one when she had hesitantly tried to question Harry about his visit.

Neither man had been specific. She glanced across and met his eyes.

'So tell me, have you bought anything for Junior yet?' He changed the subject swiftly.

She smiled tremulously. 'Actually, I am a bit on the superstitious side about that. I've put a deposit down on a pram and opened an account, but I don't want to bring anything home yet, just in case it's unlucky. I still can't believe that I'm pregnant—it seems too wonderful to be true after what the doctors told me.'

He looked across at her with a frown. 'What doctors?'

She paused. 'Do you remember that I told you I was in a car accident when I was very young?' She played nervously with her glass.

He nodded. 'When your parents died.'

'Yes...' She let out a long sigh. 'Well, I think I told you that I was seriously ill for a long time. The doctors told me when I was thirteen that I would never be able to have children.'

Josh looked shocked. He reached across and took hold of her hand. 'It must have seemed like such a miracle when you conceived. Ben must have been so happy.'

She couldn't find her voice for a moment. That last statement was so far from the truth, and it still hurt...

The contact of Josh's hand over hers set up a deep longing. She wanted his love, not his sympathy. Abruptly she pulled away.

'Well, the doctors were wrong.' She forced a bright note to her voice. 'But I'm not going to tempt fate in any way. So the majority of my shopping will have to wait until the baby is born.'

'You can always store things here if you like,' he offered nonchalantly.

'It's a kind offer; thank you.' She reached for her glass and something prompted her to add, 'But won't it upset Sophie if I do that?'

'Why should it upset Sophie?' He sounded surprised.

'Well...' She hesitated, half wishing she had said nothing. 'She might not like my leaving things around here,' she said lamely.

'I don't care if she likes it or not,' Josh said with a shrug. 'It isn't any of her business.'

'It is if you're planning on getting back together.' It took all her courage to say those words and Samantha found she couldn't bring herself to look at him. She was terrified that he would read her thoughts, see the emotive heat in her eyes. Josh was just so perceptive, and she couldn't bear the humiliation and shame of his knowing what crazy lines her mind was taking.

'What makes you think we're going to get back together?' He sat back, regarding her with steady eyes.

She managed to shrug nonchalantly. 'It's just that Sophie gave me the impression that that was what she wanted...and you said she has changed—'

'I don't think there is any way you can turn the clock back—no matter how much someone has changed,' Josh interrupted her, his tone serious. 'You can't undo the past.'

For a moment Samantha's mind flew to Ben, to the words he had spoken in the last days of their marriage. 'I realise now that I've been fooling myself about my feelings and our marriage for a long time,' he had said. 'Some men are masters at that...they can bury themselves in their work and lie to themselves... But it only works for a certain time. Sooner or later you've got to face the truth.

I can't undo the past, Sam, I can only say I'm sorry I've hurt you.'

Wretchedly Samantha wondered if Josh was lying to himself about his feelings for his ex-wife. Her heart seemed to miss a beat as she looked up and met his eyes. She didn't want to love him, she thought with anguish. She didn't want to leave herself wide open to this much pain, this much vulnerability.

'You mean you can't forgive her for her infidelity?' She put her glass down on the table and was alarmed by how much her hand trembled. She prayed Josh hadn't noticed.

'I'm not an unforgiving person. It's just that I don't think you can go back. When Sophie left she broke the trust I had in her...it would be very difficult to put that together again, act as if it had never happened.'

'Difficult, but not impossible,' Samantha said slowly, her tone uneven. 'Perhaps sometimes the knowledge of where you went wrong last time can strengthen a relationship.'

'Perhaps.' Josh picked up his glass and finished the sparkling liquid. Then he fixed her with a direct look across the table. 'How come we always end up discussing my ex-wife?'

Samantha shrugged. She could hardly tell him it was because she wanted to know the exact state of play between them...that she was torn between jealousy of Sophie Hamilton and love for him. 'Shall we move on to a lighter subject?' she suggested nonchalantly.

He grinned at that. 'World war would be a considerably lighter subject compared to Sophie.' Candlelight flickered over the handsome features, highlighting the chiselled features, the dark flecks in his green eyes.

What would it be like to wake up in the morning and look into those eyes? she wondered suddenly. The question made her heart thump crazily against her breast.

Desperately she searched around in her mind for some small talk.

'It's beautiful in here,' she remarked at last, trying to sound natural, her eyes moving around the exotic blooms on the pink and white orchids.

'It's my favourite room,' Josh replied easily. 'I thought it was fitting for us to dine in here...brings back memories of Africa, don't you think?'

'Yes.' Her voice was husky as she remembered dining with him in the Jeep—how he had made her laugh, despite the dangers around them. Then she found herself remembering the way he had kissed her, and the dangerous passions that he had unleashed inside her—dangerous because she hadn't been able to resist or control them.

Was that when this craziness inside her had started?

'I'm sorry, Samantha,' he said quickly. 'That was insensitive of me. Africa has far too many painful connotations for you.'

He thought that she was consumed with memories of Ben. 'Not all my memories of Africa are painful,' she managed to say in a voice at least approaching normality.

'No, I suppose not. You did have two years of married life together.'

Something about the tone of his voice made her glance back at him. She couldn't pinpoint what it was exactly, but there had been an edge to his words.

'Shall we adjourn and have coffee in the lounge?' he asked now, and she wondered immediately if she had imagined it.

She nodded, relieved to be away from the candlelight.

The lounge, however, wasn't much better. A log fire and subdued lighting gave it a disconcertingly romantic flavour. Samantha carefully avoided the sofa and sat in the armchair by the fireplace.

She studied the flickering orange flames as she waited

for Josh to bring through their coffee. She had to dispel these feelings for him. If he was still in love with Sophie then she was leaving herself wide open to heartache. She remembered vividly what it was like to be with a man who didn't love her. The memory sent a chill through her.

She bit down on her lip, annoyed with herself for feeling so panic-stricken. She reasoned staunchly that she didn't know for sure what Josh's feelings for Sophie were. If he was in love with his wife then why would he invite her here tonight?

Josh returned and put the tray down on the coffee-table beside her, then handed her a cup.

'Harry tells me you're settling down very well in your new job,' he said as he helped her to some cream.

'You were discussing me, then?' She glanced up at him sharply.

He just shrugged. 'No...not really. It was just a casual comment.'

Of course it was. Why would Josh be interested in talking to Harry about her?

Her heart twisted as he met her gaze. He was so attractive; his whole aura just oozed sex appeal.

She turned her attention firmly back towards the fire for a few moments.

'Did he tell you that he's invited me to go away for the weekend?' Her words lingered in the stillness of the room and deliberately she did not enlighten him and say that the 'weekend' was a computer course with six other women. Why, she couldn't have said. Perhaps it was a foolhardy way of trying to gauge Josh's reaction. Perhaps it was a sweeping act of defiance against the feelings he was stirring up in her.

When he didn't answer immediately she flicked a glance up at him.

His dark features were drawn into a frown, the sensual

curve of his lips set in a firm line. Her heart leapt in a wild moment of hope.

'Well, it's your life.' He shrugged, then perched himself on the arm of the sofa, staring at her indolently.

Her heart plummeted like an aircraft without any engines. But what had she expected? she asked herself honestly.

'I suppose it would be naïve of me to ask whether you're going to have separate rooms?' he asked derisively. 'Or perhaps you're thinking about getting rooms with a connecting door?'

'I beg your pardon?' The audacity of that statement took her breath away, and her cheeks scalded with red-hot colour as she remembered Africa. 'It was you who asked for rooms with a connecting door in the Salanga hotel...' Her voice trembled alarmingly. 'I can assure you that I would have been happier on a separate floor from you.'

'I didn't ask for those rooms,' he commented wryly. 'And, as I recall, you didn't do much complaining once you'd stepped over the threshold of my bedroom.'

'You like to keep reminding me of that, don't you, Josh?' Her eyes blazed. 'Is it a case of needing to feed your ego?'

'No, more a case of looking for the truth,' he said easily. 'And the truth is that getting involved with Harry Unwin is just going to make you feel worse.'

'Worse about what?' She glared at him. 'What makes you such an authority on my life?'

'I'm not pretending to be an authority on anything,' he said coolly. 'I'm just worried about you.'

Her mouth twisted ruefully. 'Well, I've got a maiden aunt for that, so don't bother, thank you.'

'Well, I'm not going to start reminding you to wear your slippers. My concern is more of the male variety, I can assure you.' For a moment his lips slanted in that attractive way that made her want to melt. 'You are a very attractive woman, Samantha…very sensual. As a red-blooded male I'm warning you—if you agree to go away with Unwin then be prepared…he might not be as much of a gentleman as I was that night in Salanga.'

Her face flared with colour and she put her coffee down on the table with a hand that was none too steady. 'It's none of your business anyway, but—'

'Call me old-fashioned, but because I've kissed you once…or twice…I *am* interested when you tell me that you might start seeing someone else.' Although his words were light-hearted, there was nothing insouciant about the way he was looking at her.

Confusion reigned supreme inside her now. Her breathing felt strained as she dared to hope that maybe he did care about her after all.

'I was talking about going on a computer course weekend, not sleeping with the man.' Somehow she managed to sound indifferent. It took every ounce of her acting ability.

'Well, that wasn't how it sounded,' he said grimly.

No, it hadn't been, and she knew she had purposely made it that way. Some illogical feminine streak in her had wanted to stir up some kind of feeling in him… anything—even his anger was better than nothing. Now she dared to hope that it hadn't been such a forlorn effort. 'You obviously don't have a very high opinion of me, do you?' Her voice rose.

'On the contrary, I have a very high opinion of you,' he said calmly. 'I just think you would be making a big mistake getting involved with Harry Unwin.'

'Why, exactly?' Her heart drummed against her chest as she waited for him to answer.

He glanced across at her and hesitated very slightly

before saying casually, 'Because you're very vulnerable right now.'

Was that it? Was that the full extent of his feelings on the subject? Anger and disappointment argued for first place now, and her hands curled into tight fists of futility. She couldn't stir him into jealousy because he didn't care enough.

The phone interrupted their conversation and he reached out to pick it up, his manner instantly more alert.

'Oh, hello, Sophie.' He relaxed visibly.

Samantha could feel herself tense at the mere mention of the woman's name. Was this the important call he had said he was waiting for?

'No, that doesn't suit.' Josh's tone changed subtly to a firmer one. 'Because I've got somebody here with me.' He sounded less than pleased as he listened to her reply. 'Look, now isn't a good time. I'll see you tomorrow.'

'Problems?' Samantha's voice was innocently casual as he put the phone down.

His lips tightened. 'Nothing I can't handle.'

Samantha wondered painfully whether he and Sophie were playing emotional games with each other.

'Now, where was I?' He raked an impatient hand through his hair. 'I was—'

She interrupted him suddenly. 'Did you tell Sophie that you were seeing me tonight?'

'I didn't have to. She heard me making the arrangement.'

A horrible, uncomfortable suspicion swirled in Samantha's head. Perhaps Josh was using her to make Sophie jealous. Was that the reason he had invited her to dinner?

'We were discussing Harry Unwin,' he said firmly. 'I think it would be wise to keep your distance there, Sam—'

She cut across him angrily. 'And I think you've got a nerve trying to tell me what I should and should not do. What the hell would you know about how I feel anyway?'

'I know what it feels like to lose someone you love,' he said quietly.

A tremor of pain raced through her body. She didn't want to hear how much he had loved Sophie; it was the last thing she needed.

'When my marriage broke up I went off the rails for a while,' he continued matter-of-factly. 'I dated a lot of women...none of them meant anything. No one compared with Sophie. I was lonely, I was looking for comfort—'

'Well, I'm not lonely and I'm not looking for comfort.' She glared at him, but behind the veneer of anger there was a wealth of sadness waiting to explode. She could feel her eyes prickling with tears. 'And I can assure you that my feelings concerning Ben are a lot different from what you experienced.'

'I know that Ben didn't deliberately leave you, if that's what you mean,' he said coolly. 'But you still miss your husband, don't you? That's why I pulled back from you that night when we nearly made love in Salanga.'

Her heart slammed fiercely against her ribs. The blunt statement had made her emotions tear apart. 'Well, that was very noble of you.' She got to her feet and looked over at him, her eyes clouding to a deep misty sapphire as she forced herself to continue. 'I suppose I should thank you for your consideration—otherwise I would have been just another in your long line of poor substitutes for your ex-wife.'

He frowned. 'Samantha, you're twisting my words.'

'I don't want to discuss this any further. I want you to take me home now.' She tilted her head in a proud, defiant manner, but her eyes shimmered with tears.

'Why?' He stood up slowly, his gaze moving over the

pallor of her skin, taking in the bright blue shimmer of pain in her eyes. 'Because you think I wanted to make love to you out of loneliness that night in Salanga? Is that what you really think? Is that why you have tears in your eyes—?'

'No.' She cut across him vehemently; her pride wouldn't allow an admission of such foolishness.

He moved closer to her, and her awareness of him suddenly sharpened perceptibly. The fine hairs along her skin prickled; her heartbeats increased. She knew a deep, yearning need to sway nearer, to be held against the powerful sweep of his chest.

He reached out a hand and tipped her chin up gently so that she was forced to look into his eyes. 'Just for the record,' he murmured softly, 'I wanted you that night in Salanga... I wanted you so badly that you tormented my thoughts for a long time afterwards... It had nothing to do with loneliness.'

Desire whispered through her veins at his husky tone and her heart pounded unevenly. The touch of his hand against her skin seemed to burn through her. It was enough to tip the scales of her fragile control. 'Do you still want me?' The words were spoken almost involuntarily.

The heavy silence between them was broken only by the crackle of the fire. The sound seemed to echo the fire that was blazing inside Samantha's body. It was pathetic and she knew it, but the small glimmer of hope his words had given her seemed to have stoked the furnace of need inside her. She felt its heat lick through her. She felt dizzy with longing. She was beyond pride, beyond fear.

'God, Samantha, you don't know what you're saying.' The words were spoken with the low growl of male arousal.

A curl of pleasure stirred deep inside her as she realised

suddenly that she wasn't alone in fighting for control of a traitorous hunger.

The new-found knowledge made her almost light-headed. It gave her the bold confidence to reach up and touch his face, her hand soft against his cheek, then plundering through the silky softness of his dark hair.

'Make love to me, Josh,' she whispered pleadingly. 'I want you.'

Never in her life had she asked a man to make love to her. Yet there was no embarrassment in her eyes as she looked up at him.

He pulled the heavy curtain of her hair back, watching her with narrowed eyes. 'I hope you know what the hell you're doing,' he grated roughly. 'Because you are more than mere flesh and blood can resist.'

Her lips curved in a trembling smile, then she reached and turned out the lamp on the coffee-table so that they were lit just by the red glow of the fire.

'I don't know anything,' she admitted. 'All I know is how I feel at this moment.'

He lowered his head and his lips found hers. The kiss did wild things to her body. Her hunger for him was shocking in its intensity.

He swung her up in his arms and put her down on the sofa.

A charge of electricity surged through her body. It was so powerful that it seemed to crackle in the air between them.

She moistened her lips nervously. He watched the gesture and she felt her lips burn. She wanted him to kiss her again—the desire was so strong that it was overwhelming.

His lips moved to hers. They were gentle for just a moment, as if both of them were aware that they were in uncharted waters. He groaned deep in his throat as

Samantha's lips softened in sweet surrender, then his lips grated roughly against hers, his hands moving for the fasteners on her dress.

She moaned his name as his mouth travelled downwards in a sensuous spiral along her neck to where a pulse beat rapidly, marking the quick, violent strokes of her heart.

When his hand slipped beneath her dress, stroking the full curves of her breast through the silk of her bra, her body responded with a violent surge of longing, her breasts hardening and sensitive to the point of ecstasy.

His hands stroked the soft material of her bra to one side and his fingers were cool against her heated skin. Then he bent his head to kiss one hardened nipple with slow, sensuous deliberation.

Samantha's heart slammed against her chest so heavily that she felt sure he must feel it.

Her dress was completely unbuttoned now, and his hands moved tenderly over the curve of her hips. They lingered tantalisingly at the top of her silk panties. Then he looked up at her.

The firelight flickered over his powerful features and she could see the indecision in his eyes.

'Are you sure about this, Samantha?' His voice was a harsh, abrasive sound deep in his throat. 'I want you very much, but I don't want to hurt the baby.'

Their eyes met in a silent moment of communication. She knew her pregnancy was far enough advanced for lovemaking to be perfectly safe, but the fact that he cared enough to ask made her love and her respect for him deepen.

'Just be tender, Josh,' she whispered.

That was her last moment of coherent thought.

CHAPTER TEN

THEY were lying on the sofa, their naked bodies entwined in the afterglow of passion. Samantha had drifted into sleep, but something made her open her eyes...a dream...a premonition?

Despite the satin heat of Josh's skin next to hers, and the warmth of the room, suddenly she felt cold, the glorious heat that had stolen through her body fading as she remembered begging Josh to make love to her.

She pushed the feeling of disquiet away. Josh had wanted her, she reminded herself fiercely.

Firelight flickered over his tanned, taut muscles, and she noticed again that he had a perfect body. Strong and powerful, with wide shoulders narrowing to lithe hips. He had made love to her so tenderly, so exquisitely that the very memory made a curl of desire flare to life again.

Her eyes moved over his face. The handsome features were relaxed in sleep. Her heart turned over in a sudden longing to kiss his eyelids, the sensual curve of his lips. She loved him so much that nothing else mattered, she told herself.

She cuddled closer into his body and his arm tightened instinctively and protectively around her. Reassured, she closed her eyes and relaxed, drinking in the pleasure of being so close to him.

It seemed only a few moments later that the phone rang. The noise cut across the peaceful serenity of the room, the crackle of the fire, the soft sound of breathing.

Samantha flinched, caught between sleep and wakefulness. She felt disorientated for a moment.

She felt Josh moving away from her, heard him reaching for the phone on the table next to them.

'Do you know what time it is?' His voice was low. He didn't sound annoyed, just vaguely impatient. 'OK, hold on a moment.'

Samantha pushed her hair out of her eyes and sat up, looking at the long length of Josh's back.

There was a cold wedge of fear inside her as she listened to him. Was it Sophie again?

He turned and took in the fact that she was awake. 'Sorry, Samantha,' he said softly. She noticed that he had his hand well over the receiver as he spoke to her. 'Listen, you go on upstairs to bed. First door on the right.'

His voice was gentle but firm. It was obvious that he wanted to talk in private. Her heart pounded with a mixture of anger and deep distress.

He turned away from her as she reached to pick up her clothes. She was still half-asleep and she couldn't think clearly. Her hands trembled as she buttoned up her dress. She tried to tell herself that she was being foolish. Even if it was Sophie maybe Alex wasn't well...maybe there was a perfectly reasonable explanation for Josh not being annoyed about receiving a call at this time of night...for him wanting to talk in complete privacy...

She noticed that he didn't start talking again until she was on her way out of the room, and even then his comments seemed guarded and revealed nothing as to what the call was about.

As she got to the top of the stairs she heard him getting up and closing the door to the lounge. It was then that she realised forcefully that she was kidding herself. He wasn't discussing Alex. This was a much more private...intimate exchange of words.

She leaned back against the bedroom door, and the beautiful peach and cream decor of the room blurred beneath a haze of misery. It could only be Sophie. What were they discussing at this late hour? How much they missed each other? Perhaps sleeping with her had made Josh realise that it was really his wife that he loved?

She rubbed her eyes in a fierce attempt to pull herself together, to think clearly before tears started to fall in earnest. She could be wrong...she didn't know for sure what Josh felt about their lovemaking. However, the feeling of despondency didn't lift.

She glanced across the double bed. Through a half-open door she could see an *en suite* bathroom. She was obviously in a spare bedroom, because there were no personal items anywhere. It seemed significant that Josh hadn't wanted her in his bedroom. It increased the certainty inside her that Josh regretted making love to her...that he was now talking to his ex-wife.

Her heart thudded painfully as she looked at her watch. It was almost four in the morning. If she had possessed a car she would have left without a word.

Feeling awful, she sat down on the bed. Perhaps she was wrong about Sophie, and Josh would come to her now, dispel all these uncertainties...

She got undressed and slipped beneath the sheets to wait. The minutes turned to an hour, and still he didn't come.

It was as well to face the facts now, she told herself fiercely. How could she compete against Sophie? She had nothing to offer him—nothing except her love. At the moment she did look good—her figure was still slender and inviting, she positively glowed with health and vitality. But given another few weeks, as her pregnancy became more obvious, Josh wouldn't find her nearly as attractive.

Sophie was glamorous and exciting and she had his

child. The odds were certainly stacked in the other
woman's favour.

Daylight was slanting through the open curtains as
Samantha drifted into an uneasy sleep. She awoke at
seven and was galvanised into action as she realised it
was Tuesday and she had to be at work.

She stood under the shower and tried to formulate in
her mind what she would say to Josh this morning. The
thought of facing him made her nerves stretch to taut in-
struments of pain. Obviously he regretted sleeping with
her, otherwise he would have come to her room. She
couldn't blame him. She had in all honesty thrown herself
at him.

Now she had to treat the incident in a mature manner
and admit to herself that he didn't love her—extricate
herself from the situation with the minimum of embarrassment.

She dried her hair, put on some lipstick and surveyed
her reflection in the mirror.

Her dress still looked cool and smart. At least she could
be thankful that she had chosen to wear something so
casual as she would probably have to go straight to work.
There would be no time to go home and change.

The sound of a car speeding up outside made Samantha
walk across towards the window.

A bright red Porsche crunched to a halt, dispersing the
well-raked gravel of the drive with complete disregard for
the delicate flowerpots by the front door. Sophie Hamilton
climbed out, looking elegant in a navy trouser suit. She
was closely followed by a small boy in a denim jacket
and jeans.

This was all she needed to make the nightmare complete. Samantha glanced around for her shoes but they

were nowhere to be found. Hurriedly she turned and went downstairs.

A delicious smell of freshly brewed coffee greeted her.

Josh was sitting on the sofa in the lounge, reading the morning paper. At the very sight of him her whole body seemed to go into a state of red alert.

'Good morning.' He put the paper down as soon as he heard her in the doorway. His eyes moved over her, a flicker of concern in them, but apart from that his manner was nonchalantly cool.

She wondered what was going on behind those green eyes.

His casual manner might have made it easier to forget what had happened between them on that sofa last night if it hadn't been for the gossamer-fine stockings and shoes lying beside it.

Samantha's heart slammed into overdrive. She remembered asking him to make love to her...unfastening the front of his shirt...and a wave of red-hot heat seeped through her.

'Morning.' She hoped her voice was as politely controlled as his was. 'Your ex-wife and Alex have just arrived outside.' Hurriedly she dived for the lace-topped stockings and put them in her handbag.

'Spoilsport. I was looking forward to watching you put those on.'

Josh's seductive, teasing tone sent her eyes flying to his.

The sound of the doorbell was a relief, because that outrageous statement had sent her body into a state of complete confusion.

As he went to answer the door Samantha tried very hard to come to terms with the situation and get her emotions in check.

She was just stepping into her shoes as Sophie came

into the room. The woman came to an abrupt halt and looked very displeased at the sight of her.

'Hello, Samantha, we meet again.' She pulled herself together quickly as Josh and their son came in behind her.

'Hello, Sophie.' Samantha smiled politely, and then her attention was grabbed by Alex.

He was a very good-looking little boy of eight years old, with thick dark hair and a happy smiling face. It was immediately apparent that the boy adored his father—he was chatting non-stop in an excited manner and clinging to Josh's arm as if he would never let go.

'Can we go and fly my kite today?' he was asking. 'It's breezy out there and I've brought that stunt kite you bought me.'

'We'll see,' Josh said with a smile, and ruffled the child's hair. 'Now, remember your manners and say hello to Samantha.'

'Oh...hello.' The child stopped, and like his mother he looked a little startled that there was someone else in the room.

'Hello, Alex. It's nice to meet you.'

The child looked at her shyly.

'How do you like being back in London?' Samantha asked with a smile.

'It's great.' Alex was suddenly animated again. 'I can see my dad much more often now...' Then for a moment the smile faltered. 'It will be even better when Dad comes home for good.'

'Comes home?' Samantha was puzzled by the statement.

'He has to go away...back to Africa. It's part of his job.' The little boy spoke the words as if they were a simple fact of life, but with every word Samantha felt her polite smile slipping.

The awful way she had been feeling earlier was nothing

compared with the sharp fear that stabbed through her now.

'You're going back to Africa?' Her eyes turned to Josh, wide and almost pleading with him to tell her it wasn't true. For some reason it hadn't occurred to her that he might be going back to Nuangar—not now that Alex was in London.

He nodded, and there was a grim expression on the handsome features. 'Actually, I have to go sooner than I thought.'

Alex looked up at his father, his eyes clouding, and Josh put his arm around him. His voice lowered to a gentle reassurance. 'It won't be long before I'm home again.'

'Will you be here for the summer holidays?' The child looked at him hopefully.

'I can't promise.' The rugged features were taut and it was obvious that this was hard for Josh. But even so there was an almighty anger building up inside Samantha.

It was only the end of April—how long would he be gone?

Samantha's heart went out to the little boy. He looked as forlorn as she felt. There was a part of Samantha that wanted to reach out and fold him into her arms. Her eyes blazed over at Josh, bright with fury, but he didn't seem to notice. He was watching Alex.

'Is there coffee going, Josh?' his ex-wife asked easily. 'It smells simply delicious.'

'I'll get you some.' Josh looked across towards Samantha. 'How about you, Sam?'

'I need to be at work for nine,' she answered stiffly, and glanced at her watch.

'No problem. I'll get you there,' he answered laconically. 'I'll fix us all some coffee.'

The last thing she wanted was to sit drinking coffee, making small talk with Sophie. Her mind was still taking in the fact that Josh was leaving—going back to that danger zone. She supposed dully that he was tied into a contract with his paper.

'I take it you didn't know?' Sophie said as soon as Josh and Alex had disappeared into the kitchen.

'Know?' She glanced across at her questioningly.

'That Josh is leaving.' Sophie sounded almost triumphant, as if her superior knowledge of the situation was a notch in her favour.

'No, I didn't.' Samantha felt herself growing angrier by the moment. Considering that Sophie wanted her husband back, her attitude seemed callously indifferent. 'You don't sound too worried.'

'It's his job.' She shrugged. 'We've talked it through and he's promised this will be his last trip. When he comes home next it will be for good...we're going to make a go of things then.' Sophie sat down on the chair by the fireplace and crossed her long legs, looking over at Samantha nonchalantly.

'What do you mean, "make a go of things"?' She had to ask, even though part of her didn't want to hear the answer.

'As a family, of course.' Sophie sounded so coolly confident that something inside Samantha just snapped.

'Does Josh know about this?' she asked with equal coolness. 'Because from our conversation last night it didn't sound as if he does.'

For just a moment Sophie looked taken aback, then she smiled, her poise restored. 'I know Josh still wants me. He was very upset when he told me he had to go away to Africa again. So upset his feelings slipped a little and he told me that putting his family life back together would be his first priority when he gets home.'

'Well, I asked him if you were getting back together and he didn't tell me that,' Samantha said steadily.

'He didn't tell you he was going to Africa again either,' Sophie said with a coy smile. 'I don't think he likes to upset you, Samantha. He told me about your husband. I was very sorry...it can't be easy for you.'

Samantha didn't reply. It inflamed her anger to think that Josh had discussed her with Sophie. She wondered how much detail he had gone into.

'I know Josh feels a lot of sympathy for you,' Sophie continued swiftly. 'Of course, he and your husband were good friends, so I suppose he feels it's his duty to be kind to you.'

The words were so brazen that Samantha felt a red-hot stab of fury. 'Are you trying to say that Josh is dating me because he feels sorry for me?' She turned the question back on the woman openly. Then she sat down on the sofa with an air of composure about her that she felt quite proud of.

'Does a casual dinner make a date?' Sophie batted wide eyes. 'Darling, I hate to be callous but I think you're fooling yourself where my husband is concerned.'

'You seem to keep forgetting that you and Josh are no longer married,' Samantha corrected her. 'You sound like the one who is fooling yourself.'

Sophie's eyes narrowed. 'Just because Josh slept with you last night you're imagining he's in love with you,' she hissed unpleasantly. 'In my book that's the height of naïvety.'

Samantha felt the colour leaving her face as she listened to the poisonous tirade. Surely Josh hadn't told his ex-wife what had transpired between them last night? She shook her head in silent denial. No...Josh wouldn't have done that. Sophie had just put two and two together.

Sophie leaned forward, her voice lowering even further. 'And the only reason he asked you round at all was to make me jealous. He can't forgive me graciously about Bernard, you see…he's got so much stubborn pride.'

There was a moment's hesitation and then the woman shook her head, and there was a certain amount of regret shimmering in the beautiful eyes before she continued. 'So he's talking about you and waving you under my nose just to prove a point for his masculine ego. I suppose he needs to play this game for a while.'

'Sounds like wishful thinking on your part,' Samantha said stiffly. Even as she was denying the explanation she was wondering if it was true. It had, in all honesty, occurred to her last night that Josh might be playing emotional games with his ex-wife. Had she inadvertently been caught in the middle?

Certainly Josh hadn't set out with the intention of sleeping with her last night…that had just happened. The memory made her temperature rise dramatically.

'How do you know that Josh didn't sleep with you last night just to prove a point to me?' Sophie asked, a gleam of triumph in her eyes.

Samantha looked across at the woman and her voice was clear and steady as she answered. 'Because I'm in love with him, and I know without doubt that you were the furthest thing from his mind when we made love.' That, at least, was the truth. Their lovemaking had been gloriously passionate. Sophie might have encroached upon his mind before and after, but certainly not during.

It was obvious that her answer and her confident tone had thrown the woman, because Sophie suddenly looked very disconcerted. Samantha didn't derive any pleasure from the small victory. She certainly hadn't won the war. She stood and walked out of the room before Sophie could formulate a reply—before she asked the question she was dreading. But does Josh love you? That was the question that would have defeated her utterly.

When she walked into the kitchen she found Josh and Alex sitting at the table with a large map spread out in front of them. Josh was speaking to the child in a gentle way, pointing out where he would be when he went back to Africa.

'Will you be able to send me letters, Dad?' Alex was asking, his face creased with concern.

'When I get here—' Josh pointed to the map '—and here, I just might be able to phone you. But don't worry if you don't hear from me for a while. You know it's a war area, Alex, and it's hard to get communications in and out.'

'I know.' The child nodded his head solemnly.

'But you know that I will think about you every day.' Josh ruffled the child's hair with an affectionate hand. 'And I'll be counting the days until I'm home with you.'

Samantha swallowed hard. Suddenly that stupid conversation with Sophie didn't mean a thing. Nothing was important—nothing except Josh's life, his safety.

He looked round and caught her standing in the doorway watching them. 'Oh, sorry, Sam.' He shook his head, annoyed with himself. 'I'm afraid I got sidetracked away from my coffee duties.'

'It's all right.' Her voice was low as she strove to sound composed. 'But I've got to go now, Josh. Otherwise I'll be late.'

He nodded and stood up. 'You stay here with Mum for a little while,' he said to Alex, then, turning to Samantha, he said, 'I won't be long. I'll just go and tell Sophie we're going.'

Samantha was left alone with Alex. The little boy studied her for a while and then asked in a disconcertingly straight way, 'Are you Daddy's girlfriend?'

'Well, I'm a friend.' She tried to keep her voice casually indifferent, but her heart raced nervously with the knowledge of how deeply her feelings were entangled here. She would have to take a big step backwards from the situation, she told herself severely. She was too vulnerable, and it was odds on that Josh was still in love with his ex-wife. She couldn't face that.

'Do you like flying kites?' Alex asked now, his head on one side as he regarded her seriously.

'Well, yes.' Samantha smiled. 'But it's a long time since I've done it.'

Josh came back into the kitchen and stood silently inside the door, waiting for her.

'Why don't you come with us this morning?' Alex said unexpectedly. 'It'll be fun.'

The little boy was so engagingly earnest that it was hard to refuse him. 'I've got to go to work,' she said honestly. 'Maybe some other time.'

'OK.' The child smiled.

She looked over at Josh. Part of her had wanted him to interrupt and argue with her, insist that she take the day off work, stay with them. But she understood why he hadn't. His family was his priority.

'When do you go back to Nuangar?' She was the one to break the awkward silence between them as he turned the car out of his driveway.

'Two days. I haven't got my flight details through yet.'

'Why the hell didn't you tell me you were leaving so soon?' Her voice rose slightly as she tried to contain the helpless feeling of anger inside.

'I didn't realise that it would be so soon myself.' He glanced across at her and for a moment she saw a strange expression on his face. 'There have been some new developments out there.'

'What kind of developments?' Her voice was none too steady.

He hesitated. 'I can't say too much at the moment. I'm not sure enough of the information I've received. That phone call late last night was from the central news agency in Salanga. That's where I'm going first.'

She frowned and turned to look at him. 'Are you talking about that call late last night?'

He nodded.

'I assumed it was from Sophie.' She couldn't help the bitter note that crept into her voice.

He glanced across at her and then suddenly he was pulling the car into the side of the road.

'We need to have a talk about last night, Sam,' he said seriously.

Her heart slammed against her chest. 'What's there to talk about?' Somehow she managed to keep her voice light.

'Oh, come on!' There was a hint of impatience in the deep tone. 'For one thing, I want to tell you that it certainly wasn't Sophie on the phone at four in the morning—'

'But she seemed to know all about your plans.'

'Sure I told her I was going back to Nuangar soon. I had to prepare Alex.'

'I can't believe you're going. Not after all you've said about being here for your son.' Her voice trembled with raw emotion.

'You don't think I *want* to go...do you?'

'Then why do it?' Anger shimmered in her wide blue eyes. She didn't want him to leave. The thought that he might be injured or killed was unbearable.

'I've got to, Sam. I've got a contract and an obligation to honour it...'

'You could just break it.' Her voice rose heatedly.

'No, I can't.' He shook his head, a resolute expression on his face. 'I've got a job to do and I'm a professional—'

'And to hell with your son?' she lashed out furiously.

'You know that's not true.' He took hold of her arm in a grip so tight that it hurt. 'For your information I have accepted a job offer from a London TV company so that I can be here for Alex. But I can't start until my contract with the paper is finished.'

Her heart thudded unevenly. 'You've really done that for Alex?'

He let go of her. 'Contrary to what you think, Sam, I do have my priorities in order. I didn't know that things were going to happen the way they have...' He hesitated momentarily before continuing. 'Sophie bringing Alex back was like an unbelievable dream up until last week. I think I've done pretty well to organise things as fast as I have.'

'Yes...' she acknowledged painfully. 'I'm...I'm sorry. I shouldn't have said anything—'

'Forget it.' He turned away from her.

'Sophie did tell me that you were putting your family priorities first. That you had plans for when you returned from Africa.' Every word felt heavy inside her. The knowledge that Sophie hadn't been bluffing was almost more than she could bear.

'Let's leave Sophie out of this.' His voice was ominously level, as if he was holding onto his temper or some deep emotion with the utmost difficulty. 'I want to talk about what happened between us last night.'

Now she knew why he sounded so strained. He was going to try and let her down gently. He regretted making love to her because he was getting back with his ex-wife. He just didn't want to say it like that.

Desperately she tried to make light of the situation, salvage some pride. 'I don't think we need to discuss last night. We're both mature enough to know that it didn't mean anything.'

One eyebrow rose at that. 'You mean you don't expect me to get down on one knee?' His voice was sarcastically dry.

'Men don't have the monopoly on casual flings, you know.'

It cost her a lot to say those words. The hurt she felt was buried several layers under the jovial tone. She was a past master at hiding behind a protective veneer of light-hearted remarks. She had had plenty of practice with Ben. Every time she had tried to get close to her husband's emotions she had been firmly and coldly rebuffed. The memories resurfaced vividly.

For a moment he frowned, as if her words had been totally unexpected. 'I had you pegged as the old-fashioned type,' he said after a moment's hesitation. 'Not of the ilk of "Thanks for last night and see you around some time."'

'Goes to show that you don't know women as well as you thought.' She smiled brightly, striving hard to hide the fact that he was right. To Samantha, sleeping with someone was special—it was an act of love.

The dark features were serious, the sensual lips set in a straight line as he looked at her silently.

Samantha remembered how passionately he had kissed her last night and wanted to weep. For an instant she wanted to throw pride away and beg him to take her into his arms. But her protective cloak was too firmly in place. She wouldn't allow any man to hurt her again.

'Do you know something, Samantha?' he said slowly. 'I don't believe a word of what you've just said.'

'You don't?' Her heart jumped crazily.

He shook his head. 'I don't think you've ever had a casual fling in your life.'

'Think what you like,' she muttered, looking away from him.

'You're still in love with your husband, aren't you?' he observed suddenly. 'I was right in what I said to you last night…you're still hurting.'

She glanced back at him sharply. He was so very wrong…and she wanted to tell him so. But there seemed little point. He didn't return her feelings anyway.

'I'm right, aren't I?' he persisted.

She made no reply. Somehow it seemed easier that way. She knew he would take her silence as acquiescence, and it was probably for the best. It would serve as a smokescreen for her real feelings.

'Perhaps you'd better take me to work now.' Her voice was laced with sadness, her complexion so pale that it looked like porcelain.

'Samantha…'

There was a note of regret in his voice that made her look back at him quickly.

He hesitated. She could see indecision plain on his face and it made her frown. Josh Hamilton wasn't the type to suffer from indecision…there was something she didn't understand in the depths of his eyes. 'I'm sorry,' he said finally.

'For what…making love to me?' Her voice sounded very raw.

Then he shook his head and turned away to pull the car back onto the road. 'We'd better go,' he said grimly. 'Otherwise you'll be late.'

CHAPTER ELEVEN

THE months had passed in a lukewarm haze and now London was stifling with the unusually high temperatures of an Indian summer. Samantha finished her last day of work at the aid agency and the countdown to when her baby was due started.

She tried to concentrate solely on her child. She was excited about the forthcoming birth, and while that occupied a lot of her mind at the same time she yearned for Josh's presence and worried about his safety.

Her life had felt so empty since he had left. She missed him so much that it never seemed to stop hurting. She relived each moment she had spent with him, the conversations…the passion.

The nights were the worst time. She found it almost impossible to sleep. The flat was airless; her mind was over-active.

When she finally did fall asleep she inevitably even dreamt about him. She could see the intense shimmering heat of Africa, feel the danger that surrounded him. Sometimes she would wake up, Josh's name on her lips, her heart thudding anxiously for him.

It was on a night such as this that Samantha woke up, her cheeks wet from crying, and suddenly the shrill ring of the phone cut the darkness of the room.

Immediately she thought that it might be news of Josh, that something had happened to him. Though who she thought would be ringing her, she didn't know. Still half-asleep, she reached for the receiver, blinking against the brightness as she switched on the bedside light.

There was a lot of crackling down the line and no one spoke. 'Hello?' Samantha frowned. 'Who is it?'

Still there was no reply, just a lot of interference on the line. 'We seem to have a bad connection,' she said loudly.

'Of course it's a bad connection.' A voice boomed down the line. 'What do you expect? This line is like gold-dust.'

'Josh!' Samantha almost shouted the name. She sat up in bed, shock and delight vying for the first place. 'Josh, how wonderful! Are you all right?' She hooked the phone under her ear and pushed the pillows up so that she could lean back.

'I'm fine; how are you?'

His voice sent warm tremors racing through her. She could see him in her mind's eye. The ruggedly attractive face, probably tanned to deep mahogany by now, the eyes that could melt her with just a look, the wide shoulders in a short-sleeved bush shirt, faded jeans hugging his lithe frame. Her heart turned over, and suddenly she wanted to tell him exactly how she felt about him and to hell with her pride and the consequences.

'Better for hearing your voice,' she admitted huskily, then suddenly found herself saying in a voice thick with emotion, 'Josh, I miss you like crazy. I...I keep thinking about you...'

'Samantha, are you still there?' Josh's voice cut across hers, fading and then growing stronger again as the line crackled violently.

Her heart thumped unsteadily. Obviously he hadn't heard what she had just said. Or maybe he had and felt it better to ignore it.

'Has the Nuangar agency been in contact yet?'

'What?' Samantha frowned. 'No...why?'

'Listen, Sam, I've got some news…' The line faded suddenly.

'What?' Samantha raised her voice. 'Josh, I can't hear you. What did you say?'

'I've some news—are you sitting down?'

'I'm in bed.' Samantha glanced at the clock. 'It's three in the morning, Josh.'

He swore under his breath. 'I'm sorry, Sam…this was my one and only chance to get through. Look, we might be cut off at any moment—I've had to bribe and lie through my teeth to get this line. So…'

'What?' Samantha shouted down the line as it died suddenly. 'Josh… Josh?'

There was a sound like hailstones on a tin roof, and then suddenly Josh's voice was clear again. 'Ben's alive, Sam. He's alive and he's on his way back to London.'

Samantha couldn't find her voice to answer that. She felt as if the world had suddenly gone into slow motion. She felt stunned. She felt as if she was asleep and dreaming, that at any moment she was going to wake up. Her heartbeats seemed to be pounding through her ears.

'Sam…are you still there?' Josh's voice broke into her senses like a whiplash.

'I…' Samantha swallowed desperately. 'How…?'

'Apparently he wasn't in the hospital at all when the mortar hit. He'd been taken hostage by some rebel force. They were short of medical provisions and medical help…hence the decision to attack the hospital.'

For a second Samantha was numb. 'He's alive—he's really alive?'

'Oh, yes…no doubt about it. I heard it firsthand from the doctors who treated him. Apparently he's suffering from malnutrition a little, but apart from that he's all right. You should have a letter, but you know how things are here…' The line crackled some more. 'How do you feel?'

Then he gave a dry laugh. 'Stupid question…you must be overjoyed.' There was a flat sound to the words. 'I suppose you two will be back together in no time—'

The line went dead. Samantha clutched the receiver in hands that were clenched so hard they were white. She could hardly take in what he had told her. Her husband was alive.

How long she just sat there she didn't know. Then Josh's words echoed inside her head. 'You must be overjoyed.' She didn't know how she felt…stunned was a better word. All she knew was that she would have felt better if she had had a chance to tell Josh that she loved him.

She frowned. Had Josh sounded upset when he'd asked her about her feelings? When he'd talked about her and Ben getting back together there had been a definite empty kind of tone to his voice. If he was dismayed by that fact then maybe he did care for her…maybe he had been thinking about her…missing her? Now her heart was thundering in her ears. She shook her head. She probably wanted him so much that she was reading things into their conversation that hadn't been there.

With difficulty she gathered herself together, and with shaking hands she started to dial Ben's parents' number.

Ben Walker arrived in England a week later. They had flown him into Uganda and detained him in hospital for a few days before he was pronounced fit for the long journey home. He went straight to his parents' house, and Sarah phoned Samantha as soon as he arrived.

Samantha didn't know what to do. Part of her wanted to rush around to Sarah and Edward's to see him immediately, so that she could sort things out and then get on with her life. But when she tentatively asked when it would be convenient for her to go round, Sarah was rather cool, and suggested that she wait a few days until Ben felt stronger.

It was a very delicate situation. Samantha had never mentioned to Ben's parents that they had been in the process of separating before the attack on the hospital; there had seemed little point in upsetting them with the details when they had all believed that Ben was dead. Now she wondered if that had been an unwise decision. Sarah had sounded almost hostile on the phone.

Samantha ended up making an appointment to go out there on Friday at midday.

'High noon,' Samantha muttered sardonically as she dressed for the occasion early on Friday morning. She was nervous about seeing Ben again. She didn't know what to expect. Would he have changed his mind about their baby?

She rang for a taxi, then studied her reflection critically in the long mirror. She was still carrying her baby very neatly, and the navy dress she was wearing skimmed her figure in a flattering way, so that her pregnancy wasn't immediately noticeable.

What would Ben think when he saw her? she wondered hazily. The question was no sooner in her mind than she realised very forcibly that she didn't care what he thought.

She put a protective hand to her stomach as she remembered the callous way Ben had told her he didn't want their child. She had been at a very low ebb at that time in her life, had been positively frightened of how she would manage on her own. But she had coped. One thing these last few months had taught her was that she was an independent woman; she could manage alone and she was no longer afraid.

She was glad Ben was safe, but she didn't want him back. He was just an added complication to her life that she could do without. If he had changed his mind about the baby then she would give him access to his child. That was as far as it would go. She'd rather be on her own than stuck in a loveless marriage again.

Suddenly the memory of Josh rose in her mind, of the laughing gleam in his eyes as he'd teased her about something, the way she had felt when he'd kissed her, when he'd held her in his arms. Immediately she tried to close it out.

She turned away from her reflection, annoyed with herself. She was going to have to stop thinking about Josh... She couldn't have him; he was in love with Sophie. That was the end of it.

The doorbell interrupted her thoughts and she glanced at her watch with a frown. Her taxi wasn't due for half an hour. It was incredibly early.

With a sigh she picked up her bag. It probably wouldn't matter if she was a bit early anyway.

Her landlady distracted her in the hallway, asking solicitously after her health.

'Never better, Mrs Richards,' Samantha was saying as she opened the front door and tried to edge away. Once her landlady started talking it was hard to get away, and she really didn't want to get involved today. She was so distracted, looking back over her shoulder, that she walked straight into the man on the doorstep as he started to come in.

'Steady.' A strong pair of arms enclosed her shoulders and, jolted by the shock of that familiar drawl, she could only stare up into the tanned, handsome face with shock.

'Josh! Why aren't you in Africa?'

He smiled. 'There's no need to sound quite so disappointed. It's not good for a man's ego, you know.'

She shook her head, knowing her words had come out all wrong. 'No...no, I'm so pleased to see you.' Her voice softened huskily as she looked into his eyes.

She was very close to him—so close that she could smell the tangy scent of his cologne, reach out a hand and touch him. She closed her eyes and fought the memories that flooded her mind, of Josh kissing her, caressing her.

Resolutely she stepped back.

'You're looking well,' he commented with lazy approval, his eyes moving over her with a thoroughness that made her tremble.

'Do you think so?' Her voice was tinged with shyness and she put a diffident hand to her stomach. 'As you can see I've put on a little weight since you last saw me.'

'You've blossomed,' he assured her gently. 'Pregnancy suits you.'

'Now I know you're just being kind.'

He shook his head and his voice lowered in an intimate way. 'Being kind is the furthest thing from my mind.'

The words, the look on the strongly handsome face made the ache for him inside her deepen. She knew he was just teasing her and it was the worst kind of torture.

'Seems I've just caught you,' he said as he noted the handbag on her shoulder.

She nodded. 'I thought you were the taxi.'

'Well, I can be. Where are you going?'

She paused reluctantly. 'To see Ben.'

One dark eyebrow lifted.

Conscious of her landlady standing behind her, listening unashamedly, Samantha darted a glance round at her. The woman was taking in everything about Josh, from the stylish cut of his beige suit to the handmade shoes on his feet, a look of open approval on her face.

'Can I give you a lift?'

Josh's offer brought her attention winging back to him. 'It's very kind of you...' She hesitated, wanting very much to accept. She wanted to prolong the time in his company, no matter how hopeless things were between them. Probably not a wise decision, she told herself crossly. 'I…I've already rung a taxi—'

'You can cancel it using the phone in my car.' Decisively he took hold of her arm and gently propelled her out.

'How long have you been back in England?' she asked curiously as they walked towards his car.

'I arrived the day before yesterday.'

'Oh.' Her voice was slightly flat as the thought flicked through her mind that he hadn't rushed to see her. She swallowed hard and tried to talk some sense into herself. She wanted too much.

He stopped by his car and opened the passenger door for her. 'To be honest, Sam, I phoned Sarah and Edward's house this morning expecting you to be there. I was shocked when I was told you weren't.'

'I didn't think you would be so easily shocked.' She tried very hard to make light of the situation.

'So what's going on?' His tone was abrupt, and it was obvious he didn't like the prevarication.

'Absolutely nothing.' She ignored the warning note. She wasn't about to stand out in the street and calmly discuss the breakdown of her marriage.

His face darkened, but he said nothing more and she got into the car.

She watched as he walked around the bonnet. His movements were impatient, as he opened the door and settled himself in the driver's seat. He put the keys in the ignition, but didn't turn the engine on.

She frowned, wondering why he should be so short-tempered. Why should he want to know the intimate details about her marriage? Unless, of course, he did care about her? Perhaps she hadn't been imagining things when she'd thought he sounded strained and unhappy about her getting back together with Ben?

Her heart missed a beat. She had tried very hard not to get her hopes up about that phone conversation. It was too hard to tell someone's true feelings on the phone, and she didn't think she could stand the distress of finding out she was wrong.

He looked over at her and she tried desperately to see if there was any glimmer of warmth...of love there for her. His expression was hooded. It was impossible to gauge just what was going on behind the cool eyes.

'How is Alex?' It was, in all honesty, a desperate roundabout attempt at asking about the situation with Sophie.

'He's fine.' Josh's tone was clipped. 'The good news is that I've got him back to live with me permanently.'

'You have?' Her eyes were wide and questioning; she hardly dared to think about the implications behind that statement.

He nodded. 'Sophie and I have worked things out. I'm hoping it's for good this time.'

She could only stare at him, her frail expectations turning to freezing disappointment. She had been preparing herself for this, but, even so, hearing him say it so calmly, so matter-of-factly, made her want to retreat into herself, build a massive wall around her heart so that no one could ever have the power to make her feel like this again.

'We've decided—'

She interrupted him forcefully before he could go into details. She didn't think she was strong enough to hear them. 'I'm very pleased for you, Josh.' Her voice was brittle.

He frowned. 'Pleased, but not very interested?' he hazarded in a cool voice.

'I didn't say that.' She looked away from him. 'I've

got problems of my own to sort out, and to be honest I haven't got the energy to think about anything else.'

'Problems that you don't want to tell me about?' He sounded more incensed than understanding.

She could almost have laughed aloud, if her heart hadn't felt as if it was breaking. What could she say to him? I'm in love with you and I've allowed myself to harbour just a little hope that you might feel the same way? Please make me feel better?

He swore under his breath. 'Don't play games with me, Sam. I really think you owe me some kind of explanation about what is going on between you and Ben.'

She swung around to look at him. 'I don't owe you anything.' Her voice shook with the full force of her feelings. 'You have absolutely no right to pry into my personal affairs at all.'

'At this precise moment I don't really give a damn where my rights start and finish,' he grated harshly. 'Sarah sounded bloody upset on the phone this morning. She refused to let me speak to Ben. Now I want to know what the hell is going on.'

Suddenly, in one blinding, awful moment she knew why he was here, why he seemed so angry. He thought she had told Ben about them!

It was the final insult, the final, bitter twist to send her emotions out of control. 'Now I see why you've come racing around here to see me!' Her voice was low but it was laced with bitterness. 'You know, for a moment you had me fooled. For just a second when I saw you outside my door I thought you were here out of concern for me...because maybe you gave one small damn how I was.' She laughed, but it was a sound that contained no mirth. 'It's almost funny, really, that you should think that Ben—or Sarah for that matter—should give a damn about who I was seeing...let alone who I was sleeping with.'

She shook her head. 'Well, you can relax, Josh. Your precious friendship with the Walkers is intact. I haven't breathed a word to them about our little indiscretion...but even if I had it wasn't nearly important enough to wreck my marriage. My marriage was finished long before that.'

There was a hushed silence, a silence loaded with emotion, and Samantha tried very hard to get herself under control. She was beyond reason now, beyond caring about anything any longer, except striking out against the injustice of it all.

'I think Sarah was aware of the truth behind my marriage to Ben well before even I was.' Her eyes darkened to a midnight shade of blue. 'You see, the simple fact is that the wonderful Dr Ben Walker didn't love me. He married me on the rebound from his first love, and when he discovered I was pregnant he told me our marriage was over. He didn't want me and he certainly didn't want our baby.' Her eyes shimmered now with the deep, deep pain of rejection as she admitted out loud what she had always known in her heart. 'If he was here now he would probably push me into your arms with sheer relief.'

She was aware that the expression on Josh's face had changed. He reached out to touch her and she put up her hands to ward him off. She didn't want his sympathy. She hated him...hated him as much as she hated Ben Walker at this moment, if not more.

'Get away from me.' Her voice didn't sound as if it belonged to her. Tears started to blur her vision and she looked away from him. She didn't want him to see her cry. She had her pride.

She saw a taxi pulling up across the road and the driver got out to ring her front doorbell. It was like an escape route opening up. 'We forgot to cancel the taxi,' she said stiffly.

'I'll sort it out.'

He was reaching for the doorhandle when she cut across him.

'Thanks, but no thanks. Under the circumstances I think I'd prefer to ride in the cab.'

'Come on, Sam, don't be—'

She didn't wait for the rest of his sentence. Without a backward glance she got out of his car and walked across the road.

He got out too, and called to her as she walked away, but she didn't stop.

Right up to the moment when she was in the taxi and they were pulling out into the traffic she thought Josh was going to come after her. But he made no move.

The London streets blurred through a haze of tears as she tried not to cry.

It was then that the pain struck her in the stomach. It was over almost before it began, but it shocked her nevertheless.

She frowned and put her hand to her stomach. She felt perfectly all right now—no pain, no discomfort. Perhaps it was the baby sympathising with her? The idea made her lips curve sadly.

Poor baby. No father to speak of and a mother who was in emotional turmoil. The thought was enough to make her pull herself sharply together. Her child was her priority and she would do her very best for it…to hell with everything else.

CHAPTER TWELVE

THE Walkers' residence was about an hour's drive from London. It was a regal-looking house, standing alone in the midst of a beautiful valley some two miles from Chipping village.

Usually when Samantha drove through the village she would admire its picturesque cottages with their thatched roofs and roses around the doors. It was the kind of scenery found on the front of a chocolate box. Today, however, she hardly noticed the blaze of colourful flowers or the heavy, lush appearance of the fields in the shimmering sunshine. She was trying unsuccessfully not to think about Josh.

When the taxi turned through the gateposts of Ben's parents' house a wave of surprise washed through her as she noticed Josh's car parked on the front of the gravel drive. He was just getting out, and he turned and came across to her as her taxi pulled up.

'What are you doing here?' Her voice was frosty and she could hardly bear to look him in the eye.

'You don't think I could just leave things like that...do you?' he said gently.

The gentleness of his voice was almost her undoing. She fiddled in her bag to get her purse out, trying so hard not to cry that her eyes ached.

When she glanced up Josh was already paying the fare for her.

'Here.' She tried to give him the money but he fixed her with a look of disdain.

'Don't be ridiculous.'

'Don't call me ridiculous.' Her voice rose unsteadily. 'Why on earth have you followed me here? What I have to say to my husband is absolutely no business of yours.'

The handsome features hardened perceptibly and all traces of gentleness had gone from his tone when he answered her. 'I came because I thought you might need some moral support. But if you don't want me to come inside with you I'll wait here, give you a lift home.'

'I don't want you to wait here,' she said staunchly. The more she was in Josh's company, the more she wanted him, and the harder it was to keep up her cool pretence of indifference.

'Fine, then I'll come in with you,' he said firmly.

She opened her mouth to tell him that that wasn't what she'd meant, but then the front door of the house opened and Mrs Jordan, the housekeeper, came out.

'Hello, Mrs Walker...Mr Hamilton!' the woman said pleasantly. 'What a nice surprise. Come on in. Ben is in the library. Wonderful news, isn't it?'

'Hello, Mrs Jordan. Yes, it is.' Samantha was barely concentrating. She felt as if she was on automatic pilot, her mind racing around and around. She kept wondering what Josh was playing at. He was quite obviously firmly intent on going in to see Ben with her and, short of being openly rude in front of Mrs Jordan, there seemed little she could do now.

'So...how is Ben?' she asked tentatively as they both followed the woman across the hallway.

'In good spirits, considering his ordeal.'

Samantha took a deep, shaky breath as they were shown into the library.

Ben was sitting at a desk on the far side of a large

room. Sunshine streamed through the window behind him, highlighting him and the huge crystal vase of chrysanthemums beside him. Their scent permeated the room, strong and autumnally solemn.

'Hello, Samantha…Josh. I saw you both pull up at the same time.' He stood up and moved across towards them, his manner casually easy. Obviously he thought their arrival together was just coincidental. She wondered what he would say if he knew the truth…

She was surprised by how little his appearance had changed. Although a little thinner and slightly pinched around his face he did look incredibly well, considering that he had been held hostage in rebel hands for months. His blond hair fell in a boyish way over his forehead and his skin was tanned from the African sun.

He stopped a few inches from her, his eyes sweeping over her appearance. He took in the loose navy dress and her hair like burnished mahogany against the soft paleness of her skin.

'You *are* looking well.' He extended a hand and waited for her to take it.

It seemed kind of incongruous, shaking hands with her husband, the father of her child. Yet in a way it didn't surprise her. She hadn't expected a warm welcome. Even if things in their relationship hadn't been strained their reunion would not have been ardent. Ben Walker was not a passionate man.

'It's good to see you, Ben.' Her voice didn't sound as if it belonged to her.

'It's good to be back.' He shook Josh's hand warmly. 'I heard that you drove with Samantha across Nuangar… Thanks for looking after her. It was bloody dangerous out there.'

Josh looked across at Samantha and there was a gleam in his eyes. 'It was my pleasure.'

Something about the husky, drawling quality of his tone made her pulses race. She looked away from him and sat down on the sofa behind her.

'Can I fix either of you a drink?' Ben crossed towards a drinks cabinet and poured himself a whisky.

'No, thanks.' Samantha's tone was stilted.

Josh just shook his head. He was leaning against the Adam-style fireplace, looking quite at home.

Samantha felt unbelievably tense. The situation was so uncomfortable.

By contrast Josh sounded totally relaxed as he remarked on how well Ben was looking.

'It wasn't so bad. The rebels didn't ill-treat me; they needed me too desperately.' He came back and sat in the chair opposite to Samantha. 'I bet you were surprised when you got the news that I was all right.'

'You're not kidding.' Her voice wavered—her system still hadn't adjusted to the shock. 'I didn't know you were alive up until a few days ago, when Josh rang.'

'I spent a long time in Africa, wondering if you were alive or dead as well.' Somehow from the way he spoke the words it didn't sound as if he had been worried, just vaguely curious. He took a sip of his drink then put it down. 'The last time I saw you I was being dragged out of the hospital by two guerillas and you were doubled over as if someone had hit you. I thought you might be miscarrying.'

'No.' Samantha patted her stomach comfortably. 'As you can see, our baby is still here. Alive and literally kicking.'

Ben looked uncomfortable.

That look spoke volumes to Samantha. 'I can see that you're not exactly overwhelmed by delight,' she said caustically.

He shrugged and reached for his drink again.

She regarded him for a moment as if he were a total stranger. Strange how she had never noticed the weakness about his features before. 'I'm glad you're safe, Ben, and I wish you well. We could make polite conversation for a few minutes more, I suppose, but what's the point? I've come here today to ask you for a divorce. You know as well as I that our marriage was a mistake. The only good thing to come from it is our baby.'

'*Your* baby.' He was quick to correct her. 'You know I never wanted children.' He glanced across at Josh. He didn't look embarrassed, just apologetic. 'Sorry about this... Maybe you should wait for me in the other room? This shouldn't take long to sort out, then we can have a good drink and a talk about old times.'

The expression on Josh's face was grim. 'I think I'll pass on that, Ben.'

To say that Ben looked surprised was an understatement.

'You know, it seems to me that Sarah and Edward slipped up somewhere,' Josh continued sardonically. 'Someone has obviously neglected to tell you that it takes two to make a baby.'

Ben looked angry at those words. 'Samantha knows I've never wanted kids.' He looked across at her heatedly. 'You lied to me, Sam...you deliberately told me you couldn't conceive a child.'

'I honestly thought I couldn't.' Samantha's voice trembled precariously. 'The doctors told me—'

He cut across her ruthlessly. 'Well, the fact is that I would never have married you if I'd known you wanted children.'

Samantha struggled to hold onto her composure. 'That's not what you led me to believe.'

'Look, Samantha, I know this must sound harsh but my career is the most important thing to me. I thrive on the danger and excitement. I could never be a nine-to-five man. Luckily Helen feels the same way and—'

'Helen?' It was Josh who interrupted him. 'Your old girlfriend, Helen Roland?'

'Yes...' Ben paused, as if wrestling with himself about just how much to say. 'She's here now. We're to fly out to Africa together.'

So that was why he was looking so well, why he had such a glow of happiness about him, Samantha realised suddenly.

'I never meant to hurt you, Sam.' He leaned forward, his eyes earnest. 'When she broke it off with me and married someone else I tried to forget her...honestly I did.' He raked an agitated hand through his hair. 'When we got married I thought I was over her...then her letter arrived right out of the blue—just before you told me you were pregnant. She said she'd made a mistake...that she still loved me.'

'Perfect timing.' Samantha's lips twisted wryly, then she relaxed back against the cushions behind her, her manner calm and dignified.

He shrugged. 'She was waiting here for me when I got home...I could hardly believe it.'

'I don't really want to know the details, Ben. My only concern is for my child.' Samantha's voice was crisp and unemotional. She really didn't care what he was doing or who he was in love with.

'You're different, somehow.' Ben stared at her in some perplexity. 'When I told you that our marriage was over you were so upset... I thought...well, I thought I would have a similar scene today.'

'You sound disappointed.' There was an edge of annoyance in her tone at such arrogance.

'Hardly.' He gave a dry laugh. 'I'm very happy at the moment. Helen is a brilliant doctor, absolutely dedicated.

We're discussing opening a clinic in Chuanga...' He trailed off as if suddenly aware that he was saying too much. 'As you can gather, my plans don't involve being a father.'

'It's to be hoped that Helen feels the same way about children for both your sakes,' Josh remarked abrasively.

'She does.' Ben nodded emphatically and there was respect in his tone. Then he stood up, his manner suddenly crisp and businesslike. 'I'll support you financially, of course, Samantha. I know that the child is my responsibility.' He paced towards the windows and stood with his back to her. 'But I don't want anything to do with it...I don't want to know anything about it.' He turned suddenly, his eyes bright with fervent feeling. 'Do I make myself clear?'

'Perfectly.' She also stood up, her head held high. 'But I don't need your money, Ben. I don't need anything from you. I am quite capable of looking after myself and my child.'

'Easy to say that now,' Ben spluttered angrily.

Samantha shook her head, and suddenly any anger she felt for him melted into pity. 'I am well able to manage without you, Ben.' Her voice was filled with confidence. It was a confidence that she had only gained over these last few months. She knew now her own strengths and weaknesses, and she knew that no matter how hard the going got she would manage. It was much lonelier to be in a loveless marriage than on her own. 'I'll be in contact via my solicitor.'

Ben looked startled at that. 'I suppose you will,' he mumbled bitterly. 'You claim you don't need it, but I dare say you'll want your pound of flesh money-wise.'

She laughed at that. 'You must be joking. All I want is to be free of you, nothing else. I thought I had made that clear.' She picked up her bag and headed towards the door, her head held high.

Josh didn't follow her immediately. He looked across at Ben and shook his head. 'I pity you,' he said clearly.

'What the hell has it to do with you anyway?' Ben spluttered angrily. Then suddenly his voice lifted. 'Unless, of course, you have a personal interest in my wife? Is that it? Is that why you're here?'

Samantha turned at the door. She couldn't believed the proprietorial tone that Ben had suddenly adopted. The two men were facing each other across the room, their stance very antagonistic.

'You could say that, yes.' Josh's voice was cool. He was very much in control of the situation. 'I happen to care about Samantha and the baby...I just can't believe that you are such a fool. A child is such a precious gift.'

'You're having an affair with my wife, aren't you?' Ben's voice rose unsteadily and his face was very red.

'Stop it.' Samantha cut across them. 'Stop it, both of you.' She looked at Josh and tried to ignore the ache of love in her heart. She knew he did care for her...perhaps not in the way she wanted him to, but nevertheless he was prepared to stand up for her against Ben, contrary to what she had thought earlier. His friendship with Ben hadn't been his prime reason for coming to her flat today...for demanding to know what was going on.

Deep down he must have some real feeling for her. It was just that his feelings for Sophie and Alex took precedence. For a moment her eyes misted, and suddenly she couldn't find her voice to say anything else. 'Just stop it...' she finished weakly. Then she had to turn and leave the room.

It wasn't until Samantha was out on the road that she realised she was miles from town with no transport to get her back. However, her pride wouldn't allow her to turn back to the house to ring for a taxi.

If her memory served her correctly she was almost sure there was a phone box about a mile down the road so she walked briskly along the side of the country road.

It was a hot afternoon. The heat wasn't as fierce as the African sun but it made Samantha think of the day she had first kissed Josh. Her passion had been wild and unbridled as the burning sun had seemed to sizzle through her veins. Her mind clouded. She shouldn't think about it...she couldn't love someone who didn't love her.

The sound of a car cut the silence and Samantha turned her head as it approached. Tension mounted at the sight of Josh's Aston Martin. Obviously he felt sorry for her and had decided to come after her. Well, she didn't need his sympathy. It would in all honesty probably tip her emotions over the edge of the precipice that they were clinging to.

He pulled alongside and wound down the window. 'What the hell do you think you're doing, walking out here in the middle of nowhere?'

The sound of anger in his tone made her temper rise. She had been through enough today...she didn't need him snapping at her. 'What does it look like I'm doing?' she grated sarcastically. 'Having a picnic?'

He reached across to open the door. 'Get in, Sam.' His voice was grim.

Something inside her seemed to snap. She had had enough. She needed to be on her own, away from everyone and everything.

'No...' From somewhere she got the strength to continue walking away.

'Samantha, don't be foolish.'

His voice drifted after her in the still, warm air, but all she did was increase her pace. Never again would she be second best in any man's life. If a man didn't love her completely and utterly then she wouldn't want to know him.

She heard Josh's car draw level with her, but she didn't risk looking at him. She was following her new resolution from now.

'Samantha, this is crazy. Why don't you just get into the car and we can talk?'

'I've done all the talking I want to do.'

'But I haven't.'

Still she walked on. She was feeling hot now, and most uncomfortable, but she wouldn't give in. Ahead on the horizon she could see the red telephone box at the crossroads. The sight of it was like a carrot encouraging her on.

She heard the car pull up and the sound of his door opening and closing behind her as he got out. Her mouth suddenly felt dry with a strange kind of panic.

'Samantha, will you stop for just one moment? Will you just let me say something to you?'

She whirled around, heat blazing behind her eyes, roaring in her ears. 'I don't want to talk to you! It won't make one iota of difference.'

As she turned, her foot caught in the uneven tufts of grass. One moment she was standing, the next she was falling—and falling heavily.

'Samantha!' He was beside her instantly, his hands moving over her limbs then cupping her head tenderly. 'Are you hurt? Speak to me—say something.'

'Well, I would if you would let me get a word in edgeways.' She pulled herself away from him and sat up, pushing her hair away from her face with an unsteady hand. She was lying cushioned against the long golden grasses of a meadow.

'Are you hurt?'

'Shaken but not stirred.' She met his green eyes and
then grinned ruefully, suddenly struck by how ridiculous
she must appear.

He didn't share the joke. His eyes blazed furiously and
he raked a decidedly unsteady hand through his hair.
'What on earth are you playing at? You could have fallen
out here with no one around to help—'

'I wouldn't have fallen if you hadn't turned up.'

'The way you were walking—'

'Josh.' She cut across him sharply. 'Stop fussing. Anyone would think you were the child's father. It's none of
your damn business.'

She looked away from him, aware that the atmosphere
between them was suddenly charged with emotions that
were both angry and poignant.

'If I choose to skydive from the moon—'

'Shut up, you little idiot.' He cut across her words, his
voice gruff.

'I will not. Don't you tell me—'

She was effectively silenced as his lips closed over
hers.

His kiss took her very much by surprise and heat spi-
ralled instantly. The flame of her love and desire kindled
quickly to life. She clung to him, loving the sweetness of
his touch...wanting so much more. Then suddenly she
was crying.

'Samantha...sweetheart, don't cry.' He pulled back
from her, wiping her tears from her face with tender fingers. His gaze swept over her. She was a picture of love-
liness, her dark hair spread out around her delicate face,
her eyes wide and deep hyacinth-blue.

'You know, if you went skydiving from the moon I'd
want to come with you,' he said, and his lips curved with
gentle humour.

'Don't tease me, Josh.' Her voice caught tremulously. 'Just at this moment I can't take it.'

'Who's teasing?' His eyes met hers, dark and serious.

'Don't, Josh!' Her voice rose. 'I know your sense of humour…but this isn't funny.'

She tried to sit up, but as she moved she was struck with a pain deep down inside. She gasped, and instinctively her hand moved to her stomach.

'Sam, what is it?'

His voice seemed to be coming from a great distance away as another pain struck.

Her eyes lifted to his, filled with fear. 'It's the baby… Josh, I think I'm going into labour.'

CHAPTER THIRTEEN

'CAN you make it to the car?' Josh's voice was calm and it helped to soothe her.

She shook her head. 'The contractions are—' The next pain that shot through her made her wail in agony.

'OK.' Josh stood up. 'I'll ring an ambulance from my car. Keep calm—remember your breathing.'

If the situation hadn't been so serious Samantha might have laughed.

Josh left her and she stared up at the clear blue sky, willing herself to feel better. Her baby couldn't come now—it was too early!

A warm breeze ruffled the meadow in a silky, whispering wave. The sound was peaceful, in keeping with the tone of the autumn day. Samantha felt sure that in years to come she would remember this moment. She felt at one with the universe and nature, and despite the pain she found it exquisitely beautiful.

'It's not a bad place to have a baby,' she said to Josh when he rejoined her a moment later.

'You can't have it here.' He shook his head gravely. 'There's no towels or boiling water. I've seen all the best movies, and I know you can't do anything without the accessories.'

She met his green eyes, and suddenly she was laughing through the pain.

He put his arms around her and held her. She breathed

in deep breaths, loving him…needing him. 'God, I'm glad you're here.'

His eyes moved over her face, lingering on the soft curve of her lips. 'So am I.'

'Did you mean it when you said you'd come skydiving with me?' She was trying very hard to relax into the pain, but it was hard.

'I don't think you'll be skydiving for quite some time.' He smiled and lifted her head to let it rest on his knee. 'Breathe deeply; I'll time your contractions.'

'They are getting closer, aren't they?' she asked nervously after the next few pains.

'Yes.' He saw the fear in her eyes. 'Don't worry…good job I took that course in midwifery in my last term of school.'

The statement was so idiotic coming from such a tough, powerful man that Samantha laughed through her next contraction. Half-laughing, half-crying, she turned her head into his stomach. 'Don't make me laugh—it hurts.'

'Shall we talk about something serious, then…?'

'I don't care! I don't care!' she wailed desperately. 'I'm dying—I'm sure I'm dying.'

'I won't allow you to die,' Josh said mock-sternly. 'You've got too much to live for.'

The sound of the ambulance siren in the distance was vaguely reassuring.

'Josh…' Her voice trembled. 'Josh, I want to push.'

'The cavalry are coming.' Josh stroked her hair back from her face. 'Everything is going to be all right, and you're going to have a fine, healthy baby.'

Samantha's baby didn't wait until the ambulance reached the hospital. She was born *en route*, with Josh holding tight to Samantha's hand throughout the birth.

As the piercing healthy cry of a newborn baby cut

through the tense atmosphere Samantha felt an elation completely and perfectly different from any other feeling.

'You have a lovely baby daughter.' Josh's voice was deep with emotion as he took the wriggling bundle wrapped in towels from the ambulancewoman and placed her in Samantha's waiting arms.

Samantha stared down at the little face, sweet and pink with eyes squeezed closed. She was so tiny, a miracle of life, with such perfect little hands clenched into tight fists. Samantha felt her eyes fill with tears of joy and relief. 'She's beautiful,' she whispered in a trembling voice.

'Like her mother.' Josh came closer and then folded mother and daughter gently into his arms. 'Well done, Sam,' he whispered against her ear as tears fell gently and without heed down over her cheeks.

'I love you.' She blurted the words out, and then there was a flutter of nervousness deep within as she remembered that loving him was against all the rules.

He pulled back and touched her face tenderly. Then they arrived at the hospital and there was no time for any further words.

Samantha sat propped up against the white hospital pillows. Her skin was flushed with happiness and her eyes glowed with love each time she looked down at the baby sleeping in the cot next to her.

Any minute now it would be visiting time. She hadn't seen Josh since he had accompanied her in the ambulance to hospital yesterday. She was looking forward to seeing him so much that her heart started to thunder with anticipation every time she thought of him.

She remembered the way she had blurted out her love for him yesterday and her skin burned.

Her eyes moved from her baby around the small private room. There were two bouquets of flowers on her bedside table, one from her aunt Sylvia, the other, and most magnificent of all, from Josh. Her gaze lingered on the long-stemmed roses with a dreamy kind of bliss. Red roses were supposed to be for love, weren't they? Immediately the thought entered her mind she dismissed it. She was fooling herself, storing up heartache. Josh was in love with Sophie.

Every time she heard footsteps in the tiled corridor outside, her heart slammed fiercely against her chest.

Her imagination worked overtime. Perhaps Josh wouldn't come. The thought was enough to make her feel incredibly tearful.

There was a tap at the door and she pulled herself up straighter against the pillows. 'Come in,' she invited huskily.

It was Josh. Samantha felt her heart rush in a wave of warmth and love as she looked up into his eyes.

He was wearing jeans and a blue polo shirt and he was holding a bouquet of flowers.

'More flowers?' She looked at them questioningly, her heart thumping.

'From Alex.' Josh put them down on the windowsill behind him. 'He wanted to come with me, but I told him we had some private things to discuss today.'

She watched as he gazed down at the sleeping baby, a gentle look on his handsome features. Her heart twisted as she wondered what he wanted to say to her.

'I'm calling her Lucy, after my mother,' she told him hesitantly.

'Pretty name.'

He turned to look at her then, a serious expression on his face. 'I phoned Ben this morning.'

'Sylvia told him last night about Lucy,' she said stiffly.

He nodded. 'But I wanted to know if he had any second thoughts about the baby, now that she's here.'

Her heart thumped wildly.

'The man is such a fool—' Josh's voice was harsh. Then he broke off and shook his head.

'I could have told you what his response would be.' She stared down at her slender hands as they clenched and unclenched in anger.

Josh sat down on the edge of the bed and took hold of her hand. 'Maybe he'll change his mind.'

She didn't look up. 'I don't care a jot about Ben Walker,' she said emphatically. 'But I care for Lucy's sake... He's her father.'

'I know.' Josh soothed the clenched tension of her hands with tender fingers. 'This probably sounds like the most selfish thing in the world to say,' he said suddenly, 'but I'm bloody relieved.'

Her eyes flew to his face.

'I'm hoping...' he said softly, his eyes intent on her face. 'I'm hoping that his loss will be my gain.'

For a moment Samantha's heart leapt painfully. She didn't dare to believe what he had just said. Her eyes looked into his, questioningly, lovingly.

'I love you, Samantha,' he said huskily, then his lips twisted in a lop-sided smile. 'It's quite ironic that I should tell you this here, on a hospital ward. It was on a hospital ward that I first fell for you. I feel as if I've come full circle to the most important moment of my life.'

She stared at him, her eyes shimmering.

'Well, say something.' He looked at her with anticipation. 'Did you mean what you said to me yesterday?'

'About loving you?' Her voice broke slightly.

'No, about the cost of living,' he quipped sarcastically. 'Of course about loving me.'

'I just hope this isn't a dream.' Her voice was a mere whisper.

He pinched her arm softly. 'It isn't a dream,' he assured her.

'But…but what about Sophie?' she asked anxiously. 'I thought you were back together…you said you'd worked things out…'

He stared at her then, as if she were crazy. 'Worked things out over custody of Alex,' he said firmly. 'There was never any chance that we would get back together.'

'But I thought—'

'She's gone back to Paris, Sam…back to Bernard.'

Samantha shook her head. 'I was so sure you would get back together.'

'She did seem to come back to England with that idea.' He fixed her with a steady look. 'But people are supposed to learn from their mistakes, not keep repeating them. I learnt my lesson a long time ago where Sophie is concerned.'

She bit down on the softness of her lip. 'I…I got it all wrong, obviously. But you said you missed her—'

He frowned at that. 'I said no such thing.'

'You did… You said that you went off the rails after your marriage broke up. That no woman could compare with Sophie.'

'Oh, Sam… The thing that hurt about my marriage breaking up was losing Alex. I was beside myself with grief and totally lost.' His voice trembled with feeling. 'As for no woman comparing with Sophie…that was then.' He shook his head.

'Don't you know how I feel about you? I thought it must be written all over me in capital letters. I'm crazy for you. I have absolutely no desire to have Sophie back. It's you I love. I've never stopped wanting you from the first moment I set eyes on you, and the more I tried to fight the feelings, the more they increased.'

'I never stopped wanting you either.' She whispered the

words hesitantly, her body alive with joy and a fragile new confidence. 'But I never thought you could love me... I was carrying another man's child... I'm not as beautiful as your former wife.'

'You are the most beautiful girl in the world,' he said softly, and the words were filled with love. 'Except for one, of course.'

She frowned for a second, and then smiled as his glance moved to Lucy.

When he looked back at her he leaned forward and their lips met. At first it was a gentle kiss and then, as the fire of their emotions took over, it became increasingly passionate.

'We've wasted so much time.' Josh pulled back from her, a blaze of anger suddenly lighting his eyes. 'I've been fighting my feelings for you since we first met... telling myself that you were grieving for your husband, that I mustn't take advantage of the situation. When I put you on the plane from Salanga, I thought I'd wait a respectable length of time and then look you up. Trouble was, the moment I got back to London I couldn't stay away.'

He stroked her hair back from her face and looked at her with such total love in his eyes that she wanted to cry from sheer happiness.

'It was like torture, seeing you and thinking that you were in love with Ben. You see, I knew there was a chance that Ben might still be alive early on in our relationship. I heard a whisper before I left Salanga.'

'As early as that?' Samantha looked at him, startled.

He nodded. 'I wasn't sure, and I didn't want to raise your hopes only to cruelly dash them. That was why I went in to see Harry that day. I wanted to investigate a bit further. I wanted him to confirm exactly which members of the agency were missing and where they'd gone missing.'

'He never said anything to me,' she said in a low voice.

'We didn't want to risk upsetting you in case it was wrong. We were both worried about you.'

'Harry is a nice man,' she murmured.

'Not too nice?' He tilted her head up so that he could look at her sternly. 'You didn't go away on that weekend with him, did you?'

She laughed. 'No...don't be silly.'

'I kind of guessed that, the night we made love.' Josh groaned. 'You can't imagine how I felt after I had you in my arms, kissing you...holding you. And at the back of my mind was the guilt and the knowledge that Ben *might* be alive.'

'I thought you regretted making love to me.' She whispered the words as the painful memory of how that wonderful evening of passion had ended sprang to her mind.

He shook his head. 'That phone call confirmed a lot of my theories about Ben. It was the only thing that kept me from taking you in my arms and telling you how I felt.' He raked an unsteady hand through his hair. 'That night was pure hell... I wanted to go upstairs after you and tell you exactly how I felt. But I couldn't...because I needed to know for sure if Ben was still alive.'

'I wish you had come upstairs to me.' Her cheeks flared with delicate colour. 'I wanted you so much...'

One eyebrow lifted, and there was warmth and tenderness in his eyes. 'And all that talk about how it meant nothing...it was just a casual fling?'

'Oh, Josh.' She groaned and buried her head against his chest. 'I thought that you and Sophie were getting back together. I was so desperate to cover up the fact that I was in love with you.'

'Say that again.' He held her away from him, his voice husky with desire.

'I love you...I love you.'

For a while there was no talk, just kisses so passionate that they made Samantha dizzy.

'And to think that when I arrived back from Africa I was half scared to contact you. I felt so sure that you and Ben would be back together.'

She had a struggle to compose herself enough to answer; her breathing was unsteady, her body seemed to be shaking uncontrollably. 'And all I could think about was how much I loved you.'

'If you knew the effort it took to hold on to my temper yesterday when you wouldn't tell me what was going on between you and Ben.' His voice shook. 'Hell, Sam, I wanted to drive you a million miles away. I was eaten up with jealousy, with the need to take you in my arms.'

She reached out a hand to touch his face, her heart full of wonder, full of joy that such a wonderful man could love her.

'Then, when you told me you loved me… I didn't know if I was imagining the words, I wanted to hear them so damn much.' He looked at her with deep apprehension in his eyes. 'I hope to high heaven you meant it, Sam, because I love you…you and Lucy.' He took a deep breath. 'I don't have much to offer, but I've got a son who means the world to me and a house that I hope to be able to spend more time in now that I've given up my job with the paper.'

He looked at her earnestly. 'What do you say? Do you think that you and Lucy would come and join us? Make us a family, make us complete?'

She swallowed hard, tears shimmering in the darkness of her eyes. 'It would be my pleasure,' she whispered tremulously, and reached to wrap her arms around him.

'I love you, Josh. I love you wildly, deeply... passionately.'

She clung to him, feeling the warm circle of his love around her. And she knew suddenly that she was home.

Coming Next Month

HARLEQUIN PRESENTS®

THE BEST HAS JUST GOTTEN BETTER!

#2025 THE PERFECT LOVER Penny Jordan
(A Perfect Family)
While recovering from the emotional blow of unrequited love, Louise Crighton had rebounded into Gareth Simmonds's passionate arms. They'd shared a whirlwind holiday romance... but now their paths were about to cross again....

#2026 THE MILLIONAIRE'S MISTRESS Miranda Lee
(Presents Passion)
When Justine waltzed into Marcus's office, making it clear she'd do *anything* for a loan, he assumed she was just a gold-digger. He still desired her though, and she became his mistress. Then he realized how wrong he'd been....

#2027 MARRIAGE ON THE EDGE Sandra Marton
(The Barons)
Gage Baron's wife, Natalie, had just left him, and the last thing he wanted to do was go to his father's birthday party. But it was an opportunity to win back his wife; his father expected Natalie to attend the party and share Gage's bed!

#2028 THE PLAYBOY'S BABY Mary Lyons
(Expecting!)
As a successful career girl, Samantha thought she could handle a no-strings relationship with her old flame, Matthew Warner. But Sam had broken both the rules: she'd fallen in love with the sexy playboy *and* fallen pregnant!

#2029 GIORDANNI'S PROPOSAL Jacqueline Baird
Beth suspected that Italian tycoon Dex Giordanni had only asked her to marry him to settle a family score. She broke off the engagement, but Dex wasn't taking no for an answer; if she wasn't his fiancée, she'd have to be his mistress!

#2030 THE SEDUCTION GAME Sara Craven
Tara Lyndon had almost given up on men until she met gorgeous hunk Adam Barnard. Unfortunately, this perfect man also had a "perfect fiancée" waiting in the wings. There was only one thing to do to get her man: seduce him!